Tale Of
The Four Spiders

Tale Of The Four Spiders

Kjeld Lopdrup

Library of Congress Number:		2003195038
ISBN :	Hardcover	1-4134-4460-1
	Softcover	1-4134-4459-8

This book was printed in the United States of America.

To order additional copies of this book, contact:
Xlibris Corporation
1-888-795-4274
www.Xlibris.com
Orders@Xlibris.com
23650

Contents

Chapter 1

The Fatal Detour

The date: Tuesday, June 4, 1975.
The place: Boone County, North Carolina.

The four powerful motorcycles turned off the Blue Ridge Parkway at Jonas's Ridge and followed the posted detour signs onto Route 105 north. The pavement was smooth, dry, and clean, giving the tires optimum traction. The single riders handled their big machines skillfully, and the loud rumblings from the exhaust pipes indicated that the engines were finely tuned and in top mechanical condition.

Each motorcycle was equipped with a carrier mounted behind the driver's saddle. On it were strapped various items wrapped in black plastic sheets. In addition, a molded plastic saddlebag with a hinged lid was attached on each side of the motorcycle straddling the rear wheel. The heads of the four riders were shrouded in fiberglass helmets with tinted face shields. All four riders wore leather boots, jeans, and black vinyl jackets.

After they had cleared the interchange framed by a few shops and a service station, they increased their speed. One of the drivers, wearing an orange scarf around his neck, stayed in front of the group and seemed to set the pace. His appearance was that of a self-assured man, about six feet four inches tall, muscular and built like the proverbial tailback on a good professional football team. Sitting in the saddle in a relaxed and yet erect posture, he handled his motorcycle with the delicate balance of a high-wire artist. Among his companions, he was known as "High Command" or "High C" for short, a nickname he had earned because of his daring and quick wit, his ability to intimidate adversaries, and because he usually was able to scrounge the resources needed to get his companions out of difficult situations. He exuded the impression of being one of those rare individuals that inspire respect and even deference in others, as if he was an idol or a guru.

High Command was in ebullient spirits. The sky was clear, the air temperature pleasant, and there was only a light breeze blowing from the southwest. As they were speeding down the highway, the air was pressing hard on his chest, and the jacket and jeans were fluttering against his skin. His motorcycle responded impeccably to his slightest touch of the controls. The vibrations of the engine traveled up the frame into the saddle and felt like a tingle in his spine. The roar of the wind and the sound of the rhythmic explosions inside the engine combined in his ears, muffled under the helmet. The sensations of speed and power filled his mind with intoxicating delight.

From the corner of his left eye, he saw two of his companions, "SS" and "Crazy," pulling up on his left with the third, "Firebird," trailing by only a few lengths. Instinctively, he twisted the throttle a fraction of a turn to increase the speed. He was familiar with his friends' driving habits from the many tours they had previously done together. Without being understood by the others, he shouted inside his helmet, "Hey, gang, remember that this is mountain driving! We are no longer in the flatlands. On this stretch we need real finesse!"

The formation of the four motorcycles was changing continually as they passed cars in the northbound lane or as oncoming traffic whisked by in the southbound lane. Their frequent shifting of lanes, their changing of positions, and their tailgating obviously were upsetting to the rest of the traffic, confirmed by the apprehensive expressions on the faces of many drivers as the motorcycles came streaking by.

The group roared at unabated speed through a small town in single file. The few pedestrians outside the houses looked after them while shaking their heads. Heard only by himself, High Command shouted again, "They don't know what real living feels like!" and he twisted the throttle another fraction.

Again he saw his companions pulling up in line with him, spreading out over both lanes of the road. He made the OK sign to them with his left hand, which was returned.

Their formation held together as they drove through a sharp bend in the road. The four motorcycles banked steeply while following the curvature. At the end of the bend an oncoming passenger car suddenly came into view in the southbound lane, which Crazy and Firebird were presently occupying. The two had barely time to spread apart to allow the car to pass between them as the frenzied driver was braking hard, with the sound of tires squealing. After the car had passed, Firebird and Crazy returned to their previous positions, as if nothing unusual had happened.

When High Command, a few seconds later, checked his rearview mirror, he discovered a car with flashing blue lights pulling out from the berm behind him. "Damn," he mumbled, "it looks like we've got the fuzz on our tail. Well, let'm try! They don't have a chance in this terrain." He opened the throttle as far as it would go.

The formation began to dissolve as the other riders had trouble keeping up with High Command. Reluctantly, he backed off on the throttle, just enough to keep the formation intact, while mumbling, "We've got to stick together."

With increasing discomfort, he realized that the flashing blue lights behind him were getting closer. Several oncoming cars and trucks forced Firebird and Crazy to pull back behind him in the northbound lane, while SS stayed at his left side. "Nobody is going to make me spend the night in the local slammer waiting for a court hearing," he told himself as the patrol car's wailing siren now became audible to him.

In his rearview mirror, High Command could now see the two deputies in the patrol car talking together. He checked the speedometer and shouted, "Hurry up, you guys! Is that the best you can do? In that case, get ready for evasion when I make the signal!" He intensely scrutinized the landscape up ahead for opportunities: narrow side roads, forks, crossroads, anything that could be used for diversion, hiding, or escape. For several minutes, all he could see on both sides were steep hills covered with woods, with the exception of a few winding dirt driveways leading to small fenced-in dairy farms, where they most likely dead-ended.

He motioned to Firebird and Crazy to move closer behind SS and himself where the drafts would help them to increase their speed. However, that yielded only a relatively minor gain which obviously was not enough to outrun the patrol car! Sensing the futility of his tactic, he signaled to Crazy and Firebird to return to a lateral formation, reasoning, "No sense in having them lose their nerve and give up. This formation al least ensures that the fuzz won't be able to squeeze us!"

In the rearview mirror, High Command now saw that the patrol car was trailing them by only about one hundred feet, while straddling the centerline of the road. The deputy in the passenger's seat was talking into a microphone, which he held in his left hand. In his right was a service revolver pointed at the car's roof. High Command felt hot and began to perspire.

His overactive brain suddenly remembered that he had two full bottles in his saddlebags. *If I can hit the radiator on that patrol car with one of them, it ought to put them out of commission. Or perhaps, the glass shards will puncture a tire. By now the fuzz must be preparing a roadblock up ahead! They may even begin to fire warning shots. Time is running out! Something has to be done. Now! Before it is too late!*

He reached back with his right hand and unlocked the lid on the saddlebag behind him without taking his eyes off the road. The lid opened easily, and his hand groped around inside until he felt the water bottle he usually carried with him when touring. It was a standard one-gallon sturdy wine bottle made from glass and provided with a screw cap. It was filled with water for use when they camped outdoor. His hand clutched the bottleneck and pulled it out into his lap. It was a difficult maneuver, even for one as physically strong as High Command, because of the bottle's weight combined with the turbulence of the air.

They were now traveling on a relatively straight section of the highway while driving uphill. The patrol car, still straddling the centerline of the road, was closely behind him, with the blue lights flashing and the siren wailing. Without hesitation, High Command lifted the heavy bottle by the neck and threw it over his shoulder into the path of the pursuing patrol car. Through the roar of the wind and the exhaust, he faintly heard the sound of splintering glass followed by the sound of squealing tires.

When he again checked his rearview mirror, he saw that the patrol car was quickly falling behind, while swerving wildly from side to side. It proceeded into a ground loop and finally slid out of sight over the left side of the road.

"Don't you ever mess with me!" he muttered.

His companions saluted him with yelling and making the OK sign. High Command returned their salutes with a satisfied smirk.

* * *

After eight years of service in the Sheriff Department's Highway Patrol, Lonnie Ipsen had developed into an expert driver as well as a highly professional deputy. As soon as he saw the four motorcycles speeding around the bend, he knew that their pursuit was needed. The still-warm engine of the patrol car started instantly. Ipsen steered the car onto the highway and accelerated at full throttle only seconds after the motorcycles had passed. The maximum lead the motorcycles had never exceeded four hundred yards.

Robert Tatum, a relative newcomer to the Highway Patrol, occupied the patrol car's front passenger seat. He turned on the flashing blue lights to signal that the motorcyclists should stop. When that didn't seem to have any effect, he turned on the patrol car's siren, primarily to warn other traffic of the potential danger from the recklessly speeding motorcycles. The motorcyclists kept ignoring their signals.

As they closed in on the group, the two motorcyclists that had occupied the southbound lane pulled back into the northbound lane behind the other two. Driving on this highway required special caution because of the limited visibility in the many curves and the blind spots when approaching the apex of inclines. Again Ipsen's long experience paid off, as he knew the road as well as his own living room.

The two deputies studied the reactions of the motorcycle riders. They were now within a few hundred feet, and there could be no question that their wailing siren could be heard by the riders. Fortunately, no other traffic was in sight at the time. Ipsen began to pull to the left in preparation for moving up on the side of the riders and flag them to a stop, when, suddenly, the two hindmost motorcycles again swerved left and took up positions in the southbound left lane. The motorcyclists obviously were determined to continue.

Tatum took his service revolver from its holster and asked Ipsen, "Should we try a warning shot?"

Ipsen, keeping his eyes on the road, answered calmly, "Not now, Robert. Let's check with Lilypond first."

Tatum took the microphone from the dashboard and pressed the "open" lever. Holding the microphone to his mouth, he called on the patrol car's mobile radio, "Lilypond, this is Q2. Do you receive?"

The headquarters' radio room answered immediately on the speaker, "Loud and clear, go ahead, Q2."

"Q2 is on 105 north, about four miles south of 184 intersection. We are tailing four speeding motorcycles that refuse to be contacted. Request permission to fire a warning shot. Over."

"Stand by, Q2," came the answer on the radio. The patrol car was now within easy shooting range. The two deputies watched the four riders leaning low over the handlebars. The rider on the right, who was wearing an orange scarf, seemed to be reaching for something on the right side of his motorcycle.

"Q2, give description," requested the radio.

Tatum responded, "Unreadable license plates, but from out of state, four single riders in black jackets and jeans, wearing full-cover helmets. Luggage on rear. Over."

"Q2, this is Lilypond. Do not fire warning shot, but follow at safe distance. Repeat, do not shoot unless you are being threatened. Will advise other units ahead for interception. Stay in contact. Over and out."

Tatum returned his revolver to the side holster.

Suddenly they saw the rider with the orange scarf lunge his right arm over the left shoulder. An object left his hand and came sailing in an arc towards them.

Ipsen reacted instantly by attempting to steer the car to the right of the flying object. But the time was too short. The heavy glass bottle impacted squarely on the patrol car's windshield, about nine inches to the right of his line of vision.

The patrol car's windshield was of a special design enabling it to absorb high impact forces. However, in this case, the momentum of the heavy bottle exceeded the windshield's design limit. At impact, the windshield bulged inward like a diaphragm, the glass on both sides of the reinforcing interlayer cracked from end to end, and a hole about six inches in diameter was punched at the point of impact, through which sharp fragments of the crushed bottle and the splintered windshield entered the car. Both occupants were showered by numerous glass fragments, and the visibility through the windshield was instantly lost.

Ipsen felt a stinging pain from the cuts he received in his head, throat, right shoulder, and hand, and his vision became blurred. Desperately, he stepped on the break pedal while trying to keep the car on the road by looking out through the side window.

Tatum, also feeling pain from the glass splinters in the left side of his face, instinctively pressed the lever on the microphone, which he was still holding, and shouted, "Q2 to Lilypond! We have been hit by a missile . . . going into skid . . . loosing control." On a reflex, he tightened his seatbelt, dropped the microphone, covered his head with his arms, and clasped his hands behind his neck.

Had Ipsen had his normal vision, he probably could have

recovered control of the car. However, he had to force himself to keep his hurting eyes open, and even so, he was not able to see sharply. Without him being aware of it, the car began skidding, first to the left, then to the right, before finally going into a squealing counterclockwise ground loop, while sliding towards the left side of the road. The patrol car still had forward momentum as it crossed the narrow grassy berm and rolled down a long steep bank before coming to rest in the dry ditch, the wheels spinning in the air and the siren wailing.

* * *

When the radio operator in the sheriff department's headquarters received Q2's request to fire a warning shot, he immediately telephoned the county sheriff's office.

"McClure here."

"Sheriff, this is Lilypond. Q2 is pursuing four speeding motorcycles and asked for permission to fire a warning shot?"

"Are they being threatened?"

"Not at the moment, sir."

"Inform Q2 to follow at a safe distance. Ask all Q-units to report their positions. We will need some roadblocks. I will be over in a minute. Tell Q2 not to shoot unless their lives are being threatened!"

"Yes, sir."

* * *

Bobby McClure entered the radio communication room seconds before Q2's last transmission. He heard Tatum's tense voice, "Hit by missile . . . going into skid . . . losing control . . ." A burst of static followed after which the radio fell silent.

The radio operator called into the microphone, "Lilypond to Q2. What is your situation?" No response followed. The operator repeated the message, but Q2 remained silent. Once more, the radioman called, "Q2, if you can hear me, give me two clicks." More silence. The radio operator looked up at the sheriff.

"Did Q2 report his position, Joe?" asked McClure.

"Yes, they were on Route 105 northbound. At last report, they were about four miles south of Route 184 intersection."

"Do we have the positions of the other Q-units?"

"Yes, sir. The chart is current."

"And the description of the four motorcycles?"

"On the upper part of the clipboard, sir."

"Do me a favor, Joe," said McClure. "Use one of the outside telephones and request two ambulances and a wrecker to the location of Q2. Explain the situation. Let me use your mike for a few minutes."

"Very well, sir." The operator left.

McClure studied the large county map on the wall above the radio console, and in his mind's eye, he visualized an area within which the motorcycles had to be during the next ten to fifteen minutes. He opened the microphone.

"This is McClure at Lilypond to all Q-units. I need to discuss an urgent matter with the riders of four motorcycles northbound on Route 105, spotted a few minutes ago four miles south of intersection 184. The riders are wearing helmets, black jackets, and jeans, having luggage on the rear, license plates unreadable. May be dangerous, take no chances. Q1 and Q5, proceed to Mountain View Motel two miles south of town on 105 and form roadblock. Acknowledge, over."

Over the speaker came the immediate terse responses: "Q1" and then "Q5."

"Q4 and Q8, proceed to the intersection of 105 and 181 at Linville. Acknowledge!"

In a few minutes, the sheriff had dispatched all available Q-units to seal off every paved road within a ten to fifteen minutes' radius of the four motorcyclists.

Joe came back to the radio room and reported, "Sir, two ambulances and a wrecker are on the way to Q2."

"Thank you, Joe. Now, please contact the sheriff's departments in the neighboring counties. Ask them to keep a watch on the motorcycles, just in case they slip through us. I am going to Q2. Keep me informed."

"Yes, sir."

* * *

McClure's staff car, driven by his experienced lieutenant Ron Wilson, left headquarters and headed straight for Route 105. As the car passed the Mountain View Motel, they saw that two patrol cars with four deputies already were in their place. McClure returned their greetings as his car whisked by. Wilson turned on the blue light as he accelerated.

McClure checked his watch. It showed a few minutes before 10 a.m. The car was speeding south, passing the slower moving traffic.

Addressed to the driver, McClure ordered, "Wilson, in case we spot the motorcycles, do not try to intercept them. We are proceeding straight to Q2."

"Yes, sir."

However, the motorcycles were not to be seen. At 10:14 a.m., they saw two ambulances and a dozen other cars parked on both sides of the road as they came to the peak of a long incline. Wilson pulled over and parked.

McClure ordered Wilson to put out warning flares and direct traffic. At the bottom of the long embankment was Q2 resting on its roof and a crowd of people clustered around it. He quickly descended the embankment.

The ambulance attendants were gently placing a stretcher under Ipsen, who was not moving. He was covered with blood on his face, scalp, shirt, and right hand. Tatum, still bleeding from cuts in the face and neck, and the right arm held in an improvised sling, came walking over to McClure.

"How are you feeling, Robert?" asked McClure.

"Passable," grumbled Tatum, looking askance at the stretcher. "But Lonnie took it real hard."

"That missile you mentioned on the radio, what was it?"

"I think that it was a wine bottle filled with something liquid. It was made from smoke-colored glass."

"And where did it come from?"

"The motorcyclist on the far right lobbed it. He was wearing an orange scarf around his neck."

"Could you recognize him if you saw him again?"

"I would think so. He is a big man, probably around two hundred forty pounds. Broad shoulders. The tallest of the four. I couldn't see his face because of the helmet and the face shield. But he had straight brown hair coming out from under his helmet."

"Are any of the four riders present here?"

"Negative, sir. They didn't even slow down."

"Thank you, Robert," concluded McClure. "Can you make it on your own to the ambulance? I would appreciate it if you escorted Ipsen to the hospital. Make sure both of you get the best medical treatment they can provide."

"I can handle it, sir."

"And, Robert," added McClure, "don't worry. We are going to find them."

As Tatum followed the stretcher with Ipsen on it being carried up the embankment by the ambulance personnel, a young couple came over to McClure. They introduced themselves and explained that they had arrived at the accident scene just as the patrol car was sliding off the road.

"Which way were you heading?" asked McClure.

"That way," answered the young man, pointing south.

"Did you, by any chance, notice four motorcycles heading the opposite way just before the accident?"

"Yes, as a matter of fact we did. Just before we got here. Wild guys! They were all over the road."

"Do you remember how the riders looked like?"

"Did you notice, Jean?" asked the young man addressing the woman. "I know that they were driving very fast, and they all had helmets on."

The young woman nodded. "They were pretty well covered

up. All four wore black jackets or something like that. Big motorcycles with baggage on the back."

McClure made several notes in his pocketbook and continued interviewing the remaining bystanders of what they had observed of the four motorcycles and their riders.

From the answers, he constructed a sketchy sequence of events, which indicated that the motorcycles had disappeared from view of Route 105, probably somewhere in the general vicinity of the point where Route 184 branches off to the west from Route 105.

* * *

It was five minutes to eleven when McClure returned to his staff car. He picked up the microphone and called Lilypond.

"Any reports on the motorcycles yet, Joe?"

"Negative, sir."

"Joe, there are two Q-units at each roadblock. Leave one in each place for the time being and ask them to additionally be on the lookout for suspects in outbound cars. The motorcycle riders may be hitchhiking by now. Tell the released Q-units to meet me at the intersection of Routes 105 and 184. Afterwards ask Anderson to get down here and see if he can collect some fragments from a smoke-colored wine bottle and check them for fingerprints. I will leave Wilson in charge here until the place is cleaned up."

"Understood, sir."

On the corner of the intersection between Routes 105 and 184 was a filling station in front of a garage and a small convenience store. McClure parked the car and walked over to a man in coveralls standing in the doorway.

He introduced himself and asked if the man had noticed four motorcycles passing between 9:40 and 9:55 a.m.

The answer was affirmative. He had observed a group of four motorcycles matching Tatum's description passing at a leisurely pace at about that time. They had not turned west on Route 184 but had continued northbound on Route 105.

McClure returned to his staff car, and while he was waiting for the released Q-units to arrive, he looked up at the densely wooded mountain ridges towering on both sides of the road and tried to imagine where the motorcycles and their riders might be hiding. He concluded that it had to be somewhere between where he was and maybe six miles to the north and probably very close to Route 105. There were relatively few side roads on that stretch, and they all dead-ended at a few isolated resort areas, dairy farms, and one-family dwellings. In addition, there were some scattered houses and shops along the highway itself, where they possibly could have parked. It was quite a big "haystack" to search for the proverbial needle, considering that he only had six Q-units with ten deputies at his disposal.

By a quarter past eleven, the six Q-units had arrived, and McClure briefed the deputies and outlined his search plan. Each Q-unit was to cover a one-mile stretch of the highway. They should visit all the shops and houses on their stretch, including those on the side roads, and also watch for suspicious tracks leading off the road. He would remain at the intersection, expecting periodic radio reports on their progress. He further instructed the deputies to maintain a low profile during their search.

McClure then drove his car to a clearing opposite the service station, which was being used as a parking area by the tourists who came to hike on the slopes of Grandfather Mountain. Several narrow trails, impassable even by trail bikes, led up the long mountain ridge and farther onto the next ridge to the east and on to Route 221, which twisted its way five miles distant. He noticed that there were three other cars parked in the clearing, deserted by their occupants, but there were no motorcycles. He parked his car parallel with the highway, so that he had a clear view both north on Route 105 and west on Route 184, which, after a short distance, disappeared from sight in a bend behind a hill.

The first radio report came from Anderson on the scene of the wreck after about half an hour.

"Yes, Anderson, this is McClure. Any luck?"

"Sheriff, I have picked up about a dozen medium-sized fragments and a bagful of splinters of smoke-colored glass from inside Q2 and scattered along the highway within about four hundred feet to the south. I am taking them to the lab for examination. The bottle was badly broken up by the impact; not much else is left. I also took some photos of the wrecked patrol car. Is there anything else?"

"Good work, Anderson. Ask the wrecker to tow Q2 to the garage for further examination. And, yes, how is Wilson doing?"

"Fine!"

"Ask Wilson to stay until the wrecker has finished his job. Can you give him a lift and set him off at my car at the intersection of 184?"

"Will do, Sheriff."

The minutes passed slowly. At 12:30 p.m., the wrecker, with the battered Q2 in tow, drove past his location. A short time later, Anderson's car stopped at the clearing and let Wilson out. He walked over to McClure's car.

"Any new leads?" asked Wilson as he sat down beside McClure.

"I estimate that the motorcycles should be somewhere between here and about six miles north, probably very close to Route 105. We have six units searching the area, but no leads have turned up yet. Here, have a soft drink and some potato chips."

At scattered intervals, the search parties reported their findings on the radio, all negative. It became obvious that it was going to take many hours to comb the entire target area.

"If you were one of those motorcyclists, Wilson, what would you have done?" asked McClure.

Wilson scratched his neck and thought for a minute. "From what I have heard, it seems to me that those fellows probably are equipped for camping and have some expertise in outdoor living. My guess is that they are holing up somewhere in the woods, perhaps intending to stay put until our search for them blows over. At some time, they may choose to leave one by one via different routes, probably after sundown, or within the next day or two. I doubt very much that they would try to intrude in a private home. If they did so, the risk of being discovered would be considerable. I also doubt that they would try to ditch the motorcycles and hitchhike, unless it turns out that they are stolen. That too would be too risky. If found, the motorcycles could be traced, and, furthermore, by all indications, they probably have a long way home. The motorcycles supposedly were heavily loaded, and the riders were handling them like experts, which would indicate that they had owned them for some length of time. My guess is that they are in there, not too long away." Wilson waived his arm towards the wood-covered slopes.

"What you say sounds reasonable," agreed McClure. "And where would you have turned off the highway?"

"Assuming that I wanted to take a heavy touring motorcycle several hundred yards into these woods without leaving obvious tracks, I should probably look for a small dirt road some distance away from human habitation, or maybe an access road to a farm. Heavy touring bikes are not very mobile on hillsides. I should prefer a place reasonably close to the highway with fairly level and firm ground and with a good tree cover, especially if I had planned to leave after dark," replied Wilson.

"Excellent, Wilson. You make a lot of sense. So, in your opinion, we should concentrate our search to obscure side roads on the least hilly terrain with thick patches of trees. Are you familiar with this area?"

"Not particularly, sir. I live in the town. But I know that several of the fellows in the department live around here."

"Thank you, Wilson. I like your thinking. Now, let us consolidate." McClure took the microphone from the dashboard and called Lilypond.

"Lilypond here, go ahead, Sheriff," sounded Joe's voice on the radio.

"Joe, Wilson and I are situated at intersection 105/184. Are there any problems in the county?"

"All is quiet, sir."

"Good! I want to make some changes to the Q-unit deployment. First, move the unit presently at Mountain View Motel checkpoint forward to six miles north of my location. They should continue the lookout for the motorcyclists, including suspicious hitchhikers.

Second, discontinue the remaining checkpoints and resume regular patrol duty with the units. Thirdly, ask one of the released Q-units to join me here at regular speed. Pick one which is manned by personnel who live around here, or at least are very familiar with this section of Route 105. Have it stop at headquarters on the way and bring me a large-scale map covering the area from here and six miles north. Got that?"

"Affirmative, Sheriff," answered the radio.

Turning to Wilson, McClure remarked, "It's now half past one. We still have almost seven hours of daylight left."

* * *

Finally, at twenty minutes to three, a positive lead was broadcast in the radio from Q11.

"Sheriff, we are about one and a half mile north of you on Route 105. On my right is what looks like an overgrown trail, probably the remains of an old logging road, which has not been used for ages. However, we do see some fresh tracks in the berm, which could have been made by several motorcycles crossing it recently. Shall we investigate on foot? Over."

"Stand by, Q11. You will have assistance in a few minutes," answered McClure.

Using the radio, McClure directed two nearby units to join Q11. When they had arrived, McClure radioed them to barricade the trail entrance with their patrol cars and leave two deputies at the barricade maintaining continuous radio contact. The remaining four deputies were to investigate on foot, being ready to defend themselves, if that turned out to be necessary.

The minutes passed. At 3:10 p.m., McClure asked the barricade if the party on foot was in sight.

"Negative, Sheriff," answered the radio. "The woods are very dense around here. All is quiet."

Five minutes later, one of the deputies called in. He was panting heavily, as if he was out of breath. "Sheriff, we have located four motorcycles matching the description. They are parked in the woods about four hundred yards from the highway and pretty well camouflaged. The riders appear to have left on foot. We don't see any signs of them."

"Good work," answered McClure. "Did they leave their baggage on the motorcycles?"

"It seems so, or at least most of it."

"Did you copy the license plates?"

"Yes, sir." The deputy read the numbers of the four license plates, all issued in the state of New Jersey.

"Lilypond, did you take notes?" asked McClure.

"Affirmative, Sheriff. I shall run them down at once," came Joe's voice on the radio.

"Thanks, Joe. Q11, stand by for a minute," replied McClure. Putting the microphone aside, he looked at Wilson sitting next to him. "Wilson, your hunches have been remarkably close so far. Given this new information, what do you think the motorcyclists have in mind now, and where are they?"

"Well," hesitated Wilson. "I should say that they are convinced that they are wanted by the police and are trying to devise a plan to get away undetected. They would need two pieces of information to make such a plan. First, where are the possible escape routes? And my hunch is that they are not well acquainted with this area. And second, they would probably want to have a rough idea of the size and the determination of the force looking for them. If, on the one hand, they perceive that only scant attention is being given by us, they may likely attempt to leave quickly, perhaps even this evening. If, on the other hand, they have the impression that we are breathing down their necks and have a sizable force in the field searching for them, they may choose to stay in hiding for a few days, or perhaps even hike across the mountains to Route 221 in the hope of finding some other transportation there. In any event, they seem to be confident that nobody will discover their parked motorcycles and that they can return later and pick them up. It may be a wild guess, but to me, it seems likely that they are now following the logging road to see where it ends. If it leads to the crest of the ridge, or close to it, which it probably eventually does, they may be able to get a good view of the terrain and even spot the movements of our patrol cars."

McClure studied the map of the area. The logging road was not shown on it. It had probably been out of service for forty years or more. But the map did show several hiking trails crisscrossing the mountains. In a straight line, the distance from Route 105 to Route 221 was only four or five miles, but the terrain between them was mountainous and difficult to negotiate. Still, with the proper knowledge and experience, it probably could be traversed on foot in five to seven hours. Did the motorcyclists have those capabilities? If they had just been traveling through on their way north, it did not seem very likely! And apparently, they had not bothered to take much of their equipment with them, indicating that their main intention was to return to their vehicles fairly soon.

Having pondered his options, McClure finally opened the microphone and ordered Q11 to leave the motorcycles in the same condition they had been found and to withdraw the search party without further investigation. Instead, he positioned two Q-units in hiding near the entrance to the logging road and two additional units where nearby mountain-hiking trails connected with Route 105. He decided to remain in his present position across from Route 184, where he could personally keep a watch on the entrance to the third trail nearest to the parked motorcycles, as well as being ready to join any of the other units, if anything suspicious was sighted. The remaining Q-units were withdrawn for routine tasks.

* * *

The five units, including McClure's car, which were parked within a few miles of the logging road, began waiting patiently for the motorcycle riders to make a move. They had all been placed as innocuously as possible, while still being able to keep a close watch on the most likely exit points for either the motorcycles or the riders on foot, if they should choose to leave. If the motorcyclists had been observing the highway from higher up on the mountain, it would have been next to impossible for them to detect the waiting patrol cars.

While they were waiting in the car, McClure reevaluated their options with Wilson. Searching the many square miles of wooded mountains would have required a number of participants far exceeding the capability of the sheriff's department. And, even if such a plan had been possible, it probably would have been fruitless anyway, because of the numerous hiding places available in that terrain. Also, it seemed reasonable to assume that the riders would not attempt to cross the mountains on foot in an unknown and difficult territory, unless they were absolutely pressed to do so. Their first choice had to be to return to their motorcycles and try to disappear unnoticed at some opportune time. Could they have any accomplices in the area where they might hide temporarily? It seemed unlikely but, certainly, could not be ruled out. The present pivotal unknown was if the riders felt secure enough to take a chance on returning to their motorcycles, and if so, when? All the Q-units could do for now was to wait and see.

A young couple wearing hiking outfits and carrying knapsacks exited from the trailhead at about half past four and headed towards one of the parked cars in the clearing. While they were loading their gear into the trunk, Wilson and McClure walked over and introduced themselves.

"We wondered if you, by any chance, have seen a party of four men, probably in their mid or late twenties, wearing boots, jeans, and possibly black jackets. One of the four is quite tall, well above six feet, weighing about two hundred forty pounds, and having long and straight brown hair," asked McClure.

The couple conferred, and the young man finally answered, "No, sir. We are quite sure that we have not seen anybody matching that description. In fact, it seems like there are very few people up there today. We only met with two other parties all day. In one case, it was a middle-aged couple hiking together, in the other case, two young men, about my height, wearing shorts and knapsacks. I would think that they were, at the most, twenty years old. We talked with them briefly, and they said that they were students from Charlotte."

"We do appreciate your information, thank you. Have a safe journey back." McClure looked instinctively at the license plate, which had a North Carolina registration.

By now, the clouds had built up to cover the sky almost completely, and the air was beginning to become hazy. Back in the sheriff's staff car, Wilson commented that if it began to rain heavily, the motorcyclists might choose to leave earlier than they had initially planned.

The other units stayed in contact. One reported the exiting of a local Boy Scout group at another trailhead, made up of one adult Scout leader and seven boys in their teens. They stated that they had not met with or seen anyone matching the description of the motorcyclists while they had been on the mountain. A little later, another unit reported of the exiting of a couple in their forties wearing shorts and hiking boots, and both carrying knapsacks. They too had not met with anyone fitting the description.

The first drops of rain began falling at about half past five. Daylight was beginning to fade under a heavily overcast sky, and visibility was reduced to less than a mile, leaving the highest part of the mountains shrouded in haze. The intensity of the rain fluctuated between light sprinkling and moderate showers.

It was raining quite heavily a few minutes past 6 p.m. when Wilson spotted a hiking party coming down the end of the trail while whistling the tune of "Mack the Knife" in unison. They counted a total of eight individuals, two teenage boys, three women and three men. The men and one of the boys were carrying knapsacks. They were all wearing raincoats and hats, and their footwear were thoroughly muddied. Wilson and McClure put on their uniform hats and walked to the trailhead to meet with them.

Again, McClure introduced himself and asked one of the men in the party if they had noticed anyone matching the description of the motorcyclists on the mountain. The regularly built man of about thirty years answered, "No, sir. The only other people we have seen all day up there are two young fellows in hiking outfits less than two hours ago. They were hiking south on another trail close to the crest of the mountain."

McClure quickly scanned the faces of the two other men. In the fading light and with their faces being partly obscured under their hats, identification was not easy. One was probably fiftyish, medium height and slender, clean shaven, and having a close haircut. The other appeared to be in his midthirties, having a dark mustache, perhaps a receding hairline, and a stocky body. "Thank you for the information," said McClure. "The roads are becoming very slick, so drive carefully." He turned and started walking back to his car.

One of the boys, who was carrying a knapsack, had been standing close to Wilson during the brief interview. He looked at the lieutenant and interjected, "We did see four spiders!"

Wilson repeated without comprehending, "Spiders?" Then a warm smile spread on his face, and he answered kindly, "You bet, young fellow. There are lots of spiders in these woods. I believe you! Now, you all have a pleasant trip home."

Back in the car, McClure and Wilson observed the hiking party loading their gear into the two remaining cars parked in the clearing. In short order, with their headlights on, they drove off on Route 105 heading north.

The rain was gradually turning into a heavy downpour.

* * *

When darkness fell, it was still raining heavily. Water was now running down the hillsides in muddy streams, and the visibility was down to less than one tenth of a mile. None of the other waiting patrol cars had anything further to report pertaining to the whereabouts of the four motorcyclists.

"Wilson, do you think that the riders would attempt to walk in the woods under these conditions?" asked McClure.

"Not a chance!" replied Wilson. "By now the ground is very slippery on the slopes, and the woods are too dense to walk through in the darkness. However, if they are close to their motorcycles, they may make an attempt to drive out tonight. Even that would be difficult though. My guess is that they are undercover somewhere, perhaps in a cave or below some overhanging rock."

"I tend to agree with you," said McClure. "I think that we have done all we can do for today." Picking up the microphone, he called Lilypond and left instructions to maintain two Q-units in hiding to guard the exit from the logging road and to withdraw the remaining until daybreak.

"Let's go home and get some rest," he remarked starting the car.

* * *

It kept raining until midnight, and by Wednesday morning, the air was misty. Pockets of fog clung to the hillsides and filled up the valleys. The roads were covered with water puddles and muddy streams. The sky was overcast and gray.

The mood at the morning meeting in the sheriff's department seemed to reflect the weather outside. The news of the seriousness of Ipsen's injuries had spread throughout the department, and the incident with the motorcyclists took up most of the meeting's attention.

Joe reported that two Q-units were still posted in hiding at the entrance to the logging road. Two deputies had walked into the woods at first light and found that the four motorcycles were still parked in the same place, seemingly untouched. No contact with the missing riders had been made during the night. At 6 a.m., three additional Q-units had taken up positions at the closest mountain trailheads, the same that had been under observation the day before. Highway traffic had been light, and apart from assisting a car with a stalled engine, no incidents had taken place during the night.

Anderson reported that he had found four partial fingerprints on the bottle fragments he had picked up at the crash site of Q2. They were all of poor quality but might be usable for identification.

The weather forecast called for intermittent showers in the morning, followed by clearing during the afternoon.

After the meeting, McClure went back to his office and talked on the phone to the wives of Ipsen and Tatum for half an hour. At 10 a.m., he took his car and visited Tatum at the General Hospital in Boone. Afterwards, he drove to the medical center in Charlotte to visit with Ipsen. Ipsen was under sedation, and his face was covered with bandages, making conversation difficult. Twenty minutes after he arrived, Ipsen was taken away for a scheduled eye operation, and McClure drove back to Boone.

He had expected a break in the case by the time he returned to Boone at about 4 p.m. However, nothing had been seen or heard of the four motorcyclists all day.

Before McClure went home late in the afternoon, he left instructions to maintain the five Q-units in place for the night.

* * *

It was puzzling to McClure that the situation had still not changed when he received reports at the morning meeting the following day, Thursday. The night had been clear and dry, but the motorcycles remained parked in the woods near the abandoned logging road. The few hikers that had ventured into the rain-soaked mountains had not met with anyone resembling the motorcycle riders. Neither had the riders been spotted elsewhere in the county, nor in neighboring counties.

Joe reported the only positive development in the case. He had obtained the names and addresses of the registered owners of the motorcycles. It appeared that they all came from the general area of Hoboken, New Jersey. The state police in New Jersey had no reports that the motorcycles were stolen or missing.

The weather forecast predicted continued dry and clear weather through Thursday, but a 50 percent probability for light showers during the evening and night.

At the closing of the meeting, McClure concluded, "We cannot wait forever! Anderson, please visit the motorcycles this morning and try to lift off some fingerprints. Make a few pictures too, but try not to disturb anything as far as possible. We will keep the Q-units in place until six p.m. Unless there are some new development by then, we shall cancel all stationary observation and, instead, keep intensified watch by the regular patrols. Also, if the motorcycles are still parked in the woods at six p.m., arrange to have them impounded and moved to the garage. Any questions?"

* * *

At about 4 p.m., the radio-room operator called McClure on the telephone. "Sheriff, one of the patrol cars on Route 105 just called in with some information that may be connected with the motorcyclists' case. Two hikers, who had just come down from the mountain, told the deputy that there are two dead men lying below the bluff known as 'Watauga Overlook.' They might match the description of the missing motorcyclists. The hikers said that they didn't attempt to descend from the overlook to where the men were lying, because they were sure that the men already were dead, and they thought that the terrain was too slippery and dangerous."

"Joe, please take a look on the wall map," replied McClure. "How far is Watauga Overlook from Highway 105?"

"It looks like about three miles by the nearest hiking trail. I hiked up there some years back. If you are in good condition, it will take about three hours to get up there and two hours to get down again."

"Hmm. Do you see any place that is suitable for landing a helicopter reasonably close to the overlook, Joe?"

There was a long pause in the telephone. Finally, Joe answered, "I don't see anything approaching unobstructed level ground within a mile and a half. It is rugged and steep up there, most of the terrain is tree covered. The elevation of the overlook is five thousand nine hundred feet."

"Well, that means that we can't get up there today. It's getting too late! What is the weather forecast for tomorrow?"

"Light shower activity subsiding by morning followed by clearing. Wind five to ten knots out of the west," quoted Joe.

"That does it, Joe," replied McClure. "Would you select four deputies who have at least some experience in working in the mountains. Have them ready after the morning meeting tomorrow, Friday. We will need some rope too, and have them bring their own lunches. Anderson and I, God help us, need them for a hike up to the Watauga Overlook starting at about half past nine. We will also need a portable radio telephone to stay in contact with you. Then call the National Guard and ask if they can spare a helicopter with a horse collar, you know the kind they use to hoist personnel off the ground or out of the sea. Have the helicopter standing by at the airport at one p.m. ready to fly when we call for them."

"We shall be ready, sir."

* * *

It was nearly 1 p.m. when the sheriff's party of seven reached the Watauga Overlook. The rains of the past several days had made the trails treacherous and barely passable. The drippings from the water loaded leaves, and the tall grasses, combined with their own perspiration, had saturated the clothing of every participant. Their boots and pant legs were caked with reddish mud.

In addition to the four younger deputies and Anderson, McClure had, in the last moment, accepted Wilson's offer to join them. Wilson had been with the department for nearly fourteen years, and McClure respected his dedication and valuable experience.

The overlook was facing northwest and situated just a few hundred feet below the crest of the mountain ridge. Towards the southeast, the elevation of the crest increased, albeit at a low gradient, until it peaked about five miles away. The area around the bluff was sparsely covered with spruces, pines, and thorny underbrush, which had rooted between jumbled boulders and rock outcroppings. On the northwest side, below the overlook, the face of the mountain had been sheared off, so that it dropped almost vertically for nearly one hundred feet before it merged with a long steep downward slope consisting of massive boulders and gravel, again partly covered with a vegetation of stunted spruces, twisted pines, and thorny underbrush. The surface of the overlook itself was generally leaning downward towards the northwest rim, forming a rough and craggy platform, on which numerous boulders of all sizes lay scattered among isolated rock protrusions and a thin layer of loose gravel. The size of the naked overlook was irregularly about one hundred feet in length and forty to fifty feet in width. A four-foot-diameter enclosure bordered by soot-covered rocks had been built in a relatively level area, more or less in the center of the overlook. It contained charred wood and ashes and had obviously been used by numerous previous campers and visitors.

The view from the overlook was magnificent. A long section of Route 105 could be seen in the valley ahead of them, about two miles distant. Other undulating wood-covered mountain ridges rose to the west and the north, one behind another. The overlook was a rare scenic wonder, and McClure briefly wished that he could spend more time enjoying the spectacular view. However, he forced himself to think about the job at hand.

He walked to the northwestern perimeter of the overlook to locate the two dead men that had been observed by the two hikers the day before. Deep below him, he saw a green and brown thicket, mixed with stunted spruces and pines struggling to find a precarious foothold among the rubble on the steep slope. It took him several minutes of intense watching before he discovered two human figures lying close to each other and partly hidden in the thicket below the far northeastern end of the overlook. He waved for the rest of the party to join him.

"First, I need a volunteer to climb down and scout the conditions. Be careful and look out for potential rock slides. If it is safe, Anderson will follow to investigate and make pictures."

One of the youngest deputies named Mat Mahoney stepped forward immediately. "Thank you, Mahoney," accepted McClure. "Let's tie a line under your arms."

With the other deputies holding on to the rope, Mahoney lowered himself over the rim, bracing himself with his feet against the nearly vertical rock face. Having reached the sloping ground below, he walked sideways further down to where the two bodies were lying, while still being supported by the rope. After checking the conditions, he shouted that it was safe for Anderson to join him.

Anderson tied another rope under his arms and hung the camera around his neck. With three deputies holding on to the rope and using the same technique Mahoney had demonstrated, he arrived safely at the dead men and began taking pictures with his thirty-five-millimeter camera.

While Anderson was occupied with examining the two bodies and documenting his findings, Mahoney scouted a wider area to see if there was anything else of interest. The first thing that aroused his curiosity was several pieces of clothing that lay scattered among the boulders about sixty feet further to the southwest. He called up and asked for more rope so that he could investigate.

On his way to the clothing, he suddenly noticed a pair of boots sticking out from the thicket on his left. He changed direction, and, as he came closer, he now also saw a human hand and arm protruding above the vegetation. Spreading the ground cover apart, he discovered that they belonged to a big man in his late twenties lying face down on the gravel.

"Sheriff," he called up, "there is a third body over here. I also see several black jackets or coats scattered around."

"Don't touch anything before Anderson has taken pictures of it!" shouted McClure back. "How many coats do you see?"

"Two . . . three . . . and I think there is a fourth one over there."

McClure looked surprised at Wilson. "Might it be possible that all four of them are down there? But that would not make any sense!"

Wilson nodded. "Why should the fourth have left his jacket too? We better take a close look."

"Right!" McClure shouted down to Mahoney. "Do a wider search and see if there is anyone else."

It took Mahoney fifteen minutes to locate the fourth body. It was wedged under a huge boulder about twenty-five feet away from the third body and well hidden from the overview. Mahoney called back, "I found a fourth body. He has a knife in his back!"

Wilson and McClure looked astonished at each other. "They must all have gone mad. What kind of fight could have caused this outcome? I can't imagine that it was a suicide pact! Or perhaps it was?" muttered Wilson.

"Mahoney!" called McClure. "See if you can find anything else down there. Personal belongings, weapons, anything. Comb the whole area." Addressing Wilson, he continued, "Please, would you do a search of the overlook and the ground adjacent to it? Look in particular for indications of possible outside involvement."

* * *

The National Guard's helicopter arrived at the overlook in the midafternoon to recover the four dead motorcyclists. Hovering the craft in the turbulent air above the mountain bluff was most difficult. The shifting western wind created eddies that were changing continually, and when a cloud drifted over the thermals connected to it further complicated the maneuvering.

Four times, the helicopter lowered the horse collar to Mahoney, who slipped it under the arms of one of the bodies at a time, fastened the safety strap, and signaled the helicopter to hoist. The body was then retracted through the open door in the fuselage and placed on the helicopter's floor.

By evening, the remains of the four motorcyclists had been placed in the morgue of Boone County General Hospital awaiting autopsies.

* * *

Chapter 2

The McClure's Silver Anniversary

Early June 1985.

At first there was nothing, not even the least flickering of a dream. Time itself did not seem to exist. Then a faint sound was heard somewhere in the stillness, followed by other closer ones. A soft whine? Then the feeling of foam rubber, cushions compressed, warm and moist from having supported a live body for many hours. Then awareness of stiffness and numbness materialized in the limbs and in the back, stirring the body and mind into consciousness. Finally a window seemed to open, and the light and aromas from the outside world came drifting in.

The delicious smells of warm rolls, scrambled eggs, and sausages spread through the cabin as the flight attendants began to serve breakfast. The passengers in seats 38G and 38H, and likewise in seats 39G and 39H, opened their eyes, stretched and yawned, and prepared themselves mentally for another exciting day.

Ann McClure in seat 38H raised the window shade beside her to see if they had crossed the coastline of Europe yet, Northern

Ireland to be exact. However, all she could see below was the undulating cover of unbroken gray clouds, with patches and bands of rose color showing in many places on top of it, tinted by the rising sun somewhere on the other side of the airplane. Higher up avenues of transparent clouds shimmered in a variety of deep red colors on the background of the deep blue sky.

Flight 609 had been traversing the Atlantic Ocean smoothly during the past five hours at an elevation of thirty-one thousand feet, aided by a tailwind. Having left Kennedy Airport outside of New York City the previous evening, Ann, like her husband Bobby in the seat beside her and most of the other passengers, had not been able to doze off for more than short intervals at a time.

Two flight attendants, scooting a serving cart between them in the aisle, arrived at their seats. "Would you like some breakfast?" one of them asked with a professional smile.

Ann released the tables recessed in the backs of the seats in front of herself and Bobby. "Thank you," she replied, as one of the flight attendants passed on the steaming trays.

"That was a very short night!" sighed Bobby sleepily while rubbing his eyes. "Can anyone eat at this hour?"

"Happy anniversary, Bobby," Ann countered with a warm smile. "Try it. It is very good."

Bobby McClure looked at Ann with his tired, red eyes. "Twenty-five years? Happy anniversary, Ann, and thank you for making the past twenty-five years the best time of my life." He kissed her lightly on the lips.

From the seats behind them, two familiar voices chimed in, "Happy anniversary, Mom and Dad." They recognized the voices of Stafford, their son, and Helen, his recent bride.

It was the first time any of them had been on an intercontinental flight, or on a trip outside the continental United States for that matter. With high expectations for their long-planned vacation, they had flown from Charlotte, in their native state of North Carolina, to New York the previous day to board flight 609, a Boeing 747 airplane, at Kennedy airport. Now, the fatigue of lengthy, continuous traveling was beginning to be felt, and the phenomenon of "jet lag" after a night with little sleep, and having to adjust one's metabolism to a new day beginning five hours earlier than it was calibrated for, put a damper on everyone.

It had been Bobby McClure's idea to spend their summer vacation in England and Scotland as a mutual silver anniversary gift. When he suggested it, Ann had gladly accepted. They had arranged it so that they would be able to celebrate their anniversary in a first class hotel in London this coming evening.

When they had explained their plan to their son, Stafford, he had asked if he and Helen could join them for an extended honeymoon of their own. His parents thought that would be a special treat. During the past three years, after Stafford had left their hometown to join the Forestry Agency of a western state, they had not been with Stafford very often. Consequently, they were looking forward to traveling with him and Helen for two weeks, which would also give them the opportunity to get closer to Helen.

In the early morning, Bobby remembered with fondness that bright June day in 1960 when he and Ann were married in their hometown of Boone, North Carolina. The years seemed to have flown by, but he still felt the same tenderness for Ann that he had during their courtship. His career in law enforcement had often been trying for their marriage, but Ann had been wonderfully supporting and understanding. She had worked tirelessly for his election as county sheriff twelve years later. Somehow, he reflected, she always seemed to find an inner energy to organize and help, wherever she perceived there was a need. He took her hand in his and pressed it, and their eyes met in the manner of lovers.

A pleasant voice announced on the public address system, "Good morning, ladies and gentlemen. I am Captain Godwin on the flight deck. Sorry to wake you up after so little sleep, but we do hope that you have had at least a few hours of rest and that you enjoyed your breakfast. Unfortunately, we cannot do anything about the change in time zones, which means that your night was shortened by five hours. We are now passing over the English coastline at the Irish Sea, about thirty miles west of Liverpool. We shall shortly begin our descent to Heathrow Airport outside of London, where we estimate to be on the ground in about . . . twenty-two minutes. The weather in London is mostly clear with a five to ten knots wind coming out of the west. The air temperature is a comfortable sixty degrees Fahrenheit . . . that is sixteen degrees Celsius. The local time is seven fifty-five."

The flight attendants busily collected the breakfast trays and handed out hot towels to the passengers. While the towels were hardly a substitute for washing, at least they served to soften the tired lines in the passengers' faces and wiping of their hands.

Bobby and Ann McClure were a handsome middle-aged couple, who appeared to carry their years lightly. Bobby McClure was of medium height. He carried himself erect and had quick movements, reflecting the many years he had been with the sheriff's department. Even though his body was stocky, the muscles were strong and fit. His face was ruddy and crowned by burly brown hair with streaks of gray on the sides. His blue eyes were alert, and the mouth below his prominent nose smiled readily whenever he engaged in conversation.

And yet, as Ann and his intimate friends knew well, Bobby was, by nature, a serious individual, harboring high ideals and principles. His mind was analytical. He was dedicated to his profession and to the colleagues in the sheriff's department, and he was consequently well respected. In addition, he was a well known personality in Boone County because of the visibility of his office and his participation in politics. His directness and openness, his reputation for unquestionable honesty, and the excellent morale he had fostered in the sheriff's department had also earned him the respect of the voters of the county, who now had elected him county sheriff four consecutive times.

Ann was nearly as tall as Bobby, but of a slender frame. Her dark brown hair was cut short, and her regular features and brown eyes radiated an inner calm and gentleness. She usually spoke and acted with spontaneity and with a great deal of personal charm, which made most people, with whom she came in contact, like her immediately. In temperament, she was quite different from her husband. She rarely took a strong position on any issue and seemed to find dignity and beauty in most people and situations to the point of defending and helping unrecognized causes. Even after the twenty-five years they had been married, her emotional responses were often an enigma to her rationally thinking husband.

The overcast, which had been with them most of the way across the Atlantic Ocean, began to break up. Through the scattered openings among the clouds, the picturesque and orderly green English countryside now became visible. The captain's voice once more could be heard from the cabin speakers, "Ladies and gentlemen, we are a few minutes ahead of schedule. In the landing pattern, we shall pass over London town and you should be able to get a good bird's eye first impression. Please place all bags and packages under the seat in front of you in preparation for landing. Welcome to the queen's city, and have an extraordinary day."

Below, London showed herself off in her best attire. The Thames River, full of boats, ships, and barges, shone like an oversized silver ribbon through the vast expanse of buildings, parks, and busy streets. "Look, there is London Bridge! It still has not fallen down. That over there must be the old Tower of London. And over there you can see Big Ben and the Parliament Buildings, Buckingham Palace, Westminster Cathedral!" The passengers' excited comments echoed through the cabins.

The landing was as smooth as the flight had been. At precisely 8:20 a.m., as scheduled, the big airplane docked at Gate 14A of the international flights' terminal at Heathrow Airport.

* * *

The heavily loaded taxicab pulled up at the curb in front of the Dorchester Hotel on Park Lane in the Westminster section of London. The hotel's bellboys immediately rushed out to help the arriving guests with their luggage.

The cabdriver opened the glass pane separating the drivers' compartment from the passengers' and said in a crisp Cockney dialect, "Here you are, Governor. A real nice place."

As they exited the taxi, Bobby could not refrain from asking Ann, "Do I really look like a governor?"

"Local custom," smiled Ann. "Besides, who knows, someday you may become one."

The spacious foyer in the hotel was comfortably decorated in the Old World style. While Bobby and Stafford checked in at the reception desk, Ann and Helen walked over to the tourist center to study the many brochures and maps on display. They finally signed all four up for an afternoon bus tour of the inner city, departing from the hotel at a quarter to one.

Their husbands were waiting at the elevator when Ann and Helen returned.

"We thought that we had lost you already," joked Bobby as the elevator arrived.

"No such luck," replied Ann. "We just reserved seats on a Cook's bus tour starting in about two hours. We are going to show you the town!"

"Heavens to Betsy, that's barely enough time for a shower and a nap," moaned Bobby.

"And we found out that the hotel's Terrace Room serves continental cuisine after seven thirty, followed by entertainment and dancing," added Helen. "We have reserved a table for four."

"A splendid idea," said Stafford as the elevator stopped at the sixth floor. "The champagne will be our anniversary gift."

Their rooms were located next to each other and had an extra door between them. The furnishings were in tasteful Victorian style. From the windows, they had a breathtaking view of the sunbathed Hyde Park across from the hotel, with its expansive lawns, lakes, and walkways.

Pulling the window drapes shut, Bobby looked longingly at the bed and uttered, "Don't be in a hurry to wake me up."

Ann picked up the telephone and asked for a wake-up call at a quarter to twelve.

* * *

Refreshed by the short nap and a quick lunch, the two McClure couples boarded the big sightseeing bus in front of the Dorchester Hotel. Comfortably seated, they eagerly took in the many novel impressions of London, aided by the occasional commentaries and explanations by their multilingual tour guide.

The guide introduced herself as Marjori Rianti and mentioned that she had been born and raised in Switzerland. She asked that the passengers indicated his or her preferred language for her presentation. To the McClures' relief, more than half of the tourists favored English. For the rest, Marjori alternatively spoke in German, French, and Italian.

Driving up Park Lane, Marjori explained the old traditions of the Hyde Park, which was open for the public. The McClures found it particularly interesting that anyone was free to put up a roster within a certain area of the park without previous permission and publicly voice any criticism or opinions, or engage in a debate on any subject they desired. It was a place where any amateur champion of a cause, and occasionally professional ones too, could bring their own wooden crate to stand on and try to advance his or her views for anyone who cared to listen. Usually, a curious audience would assemble around a speaker within a few minutes, although that could not always be counted on! There had never been an arrest among those who had presented their views in that fashion, even when they had been outrageous and biased in the extreme, emphasized Marjori. However, verbal heckling of an orator by his listeners was permitted!

The bus turned right on Brook Street and stopped briefly at the F. D. Roosevelt Memorial on Grosvenor Square. They continued up to Oxford Street and Oxford Circus, making a short stop at the magnificent British Museum. In the spacious entrance hall of the museum, Marjori described the enormous collections of archeological and technological artifacts, in addition to the precious paintings and sculptures displayed inside. She advised her audience to come back later and spend a full day to get even a limited impression of them.

Back on the bus, they drove through the quaint historic sections of inner London with their marketplaces and the stock exchange before making a stop at the Tower of London. Leading the group of tourists into the massive fortress, Marjori outlined how the original White Tower in the center of the grounds had been built by the Norman invaders in the eleventh century under the direction of William I. Over the years, walls and additional towers and moats had been added in many stages, making it virtually impenetrable against attackers. Originally built as a royal residence, it was later used by the Royal Mint and the Royal Menagerie, and as storage of public records, an observatory, and an armory. The public probably remembers it best as the crown's prison for offenders of the state. Marjorie guided the group inside the fortress to show them the collections of armaments and uniforms going back to medieval times, the priceless collection of the royal family's crown jewels, the old prison cells and torture chambers, including the many horrible contraptions designed to extract confessions from hapless prisoners.

After about an hour in the fortress, the group was seated in the bus again. They now drove south across the old Tower Bridge spanning the Thames River, over to Blackfriars Road and crossed the Thames once more before turning west on the picturesque Victoria Embankment.

The bus stopped again at the famous Madame Tussaud's Wax Museum. The group went inside to see the life-size and lifelike wax copies of numerous well-known personalities, many still living. The long list of names included many members of the royal families, politicians, actors, military heroes, and even notorious criminals. Bobby McClure studied with particular interest the 'Chamber of Horror,' including displays depicting the legendary Jack the Ripper committing one of his murders in a narrow London alley, and another montage next to it showing the fictitious private detective Sherlock Holmes working with his friend Dr. Watson.

Back on the bus, they passed the Victoria Embankment Gardens, drove up to Trafalgar Square and on to the Parliament Square, where the bus parked. Once more they got out to visit the historic and architecturally beautiful Houses of the Parliament and Westminster Abbey under the never-stopping Big Ben clock.

In the late afternoon, they passed by St. James Park and stopped briefly in front of Buckingham Palace, the residence of the family of the English monarch. It was past 6 p.m. when the bus returned to the Dorchester Hotel.

* * *

The elegant Terrace Room on the top floor of the Dorchester Hotel was nearly full when the two McClure couples dressed in evening clothes arrived by the elevator. A tuxedo-clad head waiter received them in the foyer and checked their names off the list of reservations. He welcomed them courteously and escorted them to a table a few rows back from the elevated stage and adjacent to the currently empty dancing floor. Having helped them to take their seats, he took orders for drinks.

A band was occupying the stage and playing soft dinner music. The room was decorated in empire style, with columns, beams, panels, and window frames in dark oak wood. The crystal chandeliers spread a pleasantly soft light. The tables had been set on a starched white table cloth with a blue and red center cloth, on which a vase with freshly cut flowers was placed. The polished silverware, china, crystal glasses, and folded napkins for four were immaculately arranged.

When the drinks had been served, Bobby lifted his glass and asked, "May I propose a toast for all brides, and especially for Stafford's and mine, thanking them for having selected such an exquisite place for celebrating this memorable evening."

"Hear, hear! I will drink to that," replied Stafford, winking at Helen.

After the first toast, Helen lifted her glass. "May Stafford and I propose another toast for the silver wedding anniversary couple. We both hope that we will look as dashing and be as happy and content as you are tonight when we have been married for twenty-five years."

"I am sure you will, darling, thank you," replied Ann, touched.

The many impressions and events of the past twenty-four hours prompted a rich supply of topics for recounting and comparisons among the four of them. They were deeply engaged in busy and lighthearted talking when the waiter asked if they were ready to order their meal.

Following much debate, the whole party ordered, upon recommendation by the knowledgeable waiter, Vichy Soice, Poulard Cordon Bleu, served with small new potatoes and cauliflowers, a parsley gravy, and for desert, strawberry cake with whipped cream and cafe noir. In addition, Stafford ordered a bottle of French champagne to be served with the entree.

Their conversation continued lively throughout the delicious meal. Even Helen, whom Bobby and Ann had not before spent much personal time with, loosened up and participated as if she had been in the family for years by the time the strawberry cake was being served.

* * *

Chapter 3

Señor Fontini's Performance

Shortly before 9 p.m., the band stopped playing and vacated the stage. A couple of stagehands were in the process of rearranging the furnishings and microphones, while the waiters busily cleaned the tables. A little later, an announcer walked onto the stage and took hold of one of the microphones.

"Good evening, ladies and gentlemen, and again welcome to the Terrace Room. For your entertainment tonight, the Dorchester Hotel is proud to present yet another performance by the world-renowned illusionist and hypnotist, Señor Fontini, who will demonstrate examples of his remarkable knowledge of the human mind and behavior. Please welcome, Señor Fontini and his lovely assistant."

It was clear to the McClures that Señor Fontini had to be a popular entertainer here based on the warm applause, which greeted his and his assistant's arrival on the stage.

Señor Fontini was slender and slightly above average in height. He appeared to be in his mid to late fifties and obviously had kept himself in excellent physical condition. His hair was thinning, and there was a significant amount of gray among the brown. Alert blue eyes and a narrow mustache dominated his smooth face. He looked distinguished in a suit of black tails combined with shining black shoes, and he smiled warmly to the audience as he made several short bows. His assistant in a silver-colored long evening dress remained in the background.

During the applause, Bobby McClure leaned over to Ann and asked, "Have we not seen him somewhere before?"

"Not that I remember," replied Ann. "Where could that have been?"

"I don't know, but there seems to be something familiar about him," insisted Bobby.

Señor Fontini lifted his hands for silence and began speaking.

"Thank you . . . thank you very much. You are being very kind. We really enjoy being back in London again, and particularly being here in this beautiful Terrace Room. Some of you may remember us from previous years' performances. For others, it may be the first time we meet. Let me, therefore, begin with introducing my indispensable assistant Miss Fogelsang, without whom my performances would be severely handicapped."

After the polite applause, he continued, "In my introduction, I should also like to emphasize that my arts have nothing to do with the occult or the supernatural. They are based solely on facts and natural phenomena, some of which admittedly may not be widely known, as yet. I might add, fortunately! Otherwise, I probably should be out of a job. Why don't we start tonight with a demonstration of the power of suggestion involving the senses of taste, smell, and sight."

He walked to a table on the stage, on which was placed several empty wine glasses and a transparent glass pitcher. His assistant handed him the pitcher, which he held up for everyone to see. "I believe that you will all agree that this pitcher is filled with plain, clean tap water?"

A doubting voice was heard from someone in the room.

"Someone is not convinced, I think. Miss Fogelsang, would you please take a glass to the gentleman and let him sample the water?" Fontini poured some of the content from the pitcher into one of the glasses. The assistant went down from the stage and brought it to the table of the questioning gentleman.

After looking curiously at the contents, he twirled and sniffed the glass. Finally, he took several sips before he grudgingly admitted that, as far as he could tell, it was indeed ordinary tap water.

"Are there anyone else who would like to taste it?" asked Fontini. Nobody reacted. "Very well. We have now confirmed that the content of the pitcher looks and tastes like ordinary fresh water. I wonder if we may have someone in the audience who enjoys a particular kind of wine?"

Several hands were raised immediately. Fontini pointed to a lady and asked, "Would you mind to join us on the stage?"

The middle-aged lady came up and introduced herself as Mrs. Dorothy Wright. "Mrs. Wright," asked Fontini, "which is your favorite wine?"

"I just adore Liebfrauenmilch," she replied.

"Excellent choice! And how sweet do you prefer it to be?"

"Just a little on the sweet side, but not overly sweet."

"I do believe that I understand what your preference is, and I shall do the best I can," replied Señor Fontini while making eye contact with her. Placing one hand under the bottom of the pitcher and the other over its top, he proceeded to make a full turn. He then held the pitcher up with his right hand and straightened his arm in full view of the audience. The clear liquid in the pitcher turned to a pale golden color, the natural color of Liebfrauenmilch wine!

The assistant handed him an empty glass, and Señor Fontini poured it half full from the pitcher. Handing it to Mrs. Wright, he asked, "And how would you judge the product of this selection?"

Mrs. Wright took the glass, sniffed it and took a small sip. Having tasted it, she looked surprised and took a bigger second sip. "Indeed," she said, "this is an excellent Liebfrauenmilch." She emptied the glass during the applause.

"Thank you very much, Mrs. Wright. Is there someone else with a preference? Yes, sir." Fontini pointed to an elderly gentleman with an impressive handlebar mustache clamoring to attract his attention.

Introducing himself as Mr. J. T. N. Marlborough III, he rasped that his favorite wine was Haut-Medoc Chateau Latour Bordeaux wine, preferably vintage 1977.

Señor Fontini swallowed hard in staged consternation and clowned a little for the audience. "Do you know, sir, what a bottle of that wine is selling for?" he asked.

"Plenty, if you are lucky enough to find any," retorted Mr. Marlborough with a brusque laughter.

"Obviously, Mr. Marlborough is quite a wine connoisseur. We may need a little extra care this time," warned Fontini, looking at the elderly gentleman. "Now, let us see. Chateau Latour 1977? Yes, it was definitely a very good year. I enjoyed that one too."

Again he took the pitcher between his hands, made a full turn and held it out towards the audience. The previously pale golden liquid now turned into a dark burgundy color!

Receiving a clean wine glass from his assistant, Señor Fontini poured a sample from the pitcher and handed it to Mr. Marlborough.

After swirling the glass and sniffing it several times, Mr. Marlborough lifted it up against the light. He then took small sips repeatedly. "By Jove," he finally admitted, looking very confused, "it does look, taste, and smell exactly like a 1977 Chateau Latour. Remarkable!"

"Thank you. Coming from you, Mr. Marlborough, I consider that quite a compliment! Now, is there one last choice?"

Fontini pointed to a man in a business suit, who came up and stated that his favorite wine was Mateus Rose. Fontini then followed the same procedure he had used before, and the color of the content of the pincher now turned to a paler red in front of the audience's eyes. The gentleman affirmed after his tasting that in his judgment it was indistinguishable from Mateus Rose wine.

At the end of the act, Fontini had the liquid in the pitcher turn clear again. When the assistant brought a glass with a sample of the content to the same gentleman, who earlier had insisted on proof, he once more confirmed that it was just ordinary tap water without any aftertaste.

Fontini's act had been delivered with showmanship, wit, and elegance, and the audience rewarded him with a lengthy applause.

* * *

During the short intermission, the stagehands rearranged the furnishings on the stage, and Bobby McClure again found himself wondering if he had previously seen Señor Fontini. He concluded that it could not have been at a public performance, as he had never before attended a similar illusionist show. Still, there was something in that profile, the strong blue eyes and the movements that reminded him of someone he had met in the past. At last he pushed the thought out of his mind, deciding that it must be a case of deja vu or doppelgangers.

Señor Fontini and his assistant entered the stage again. "In the second part of our performance tonight, we shall demonstrate telepathy or, as some prefer to label it, transfer of thoughts. Because telepathy requires an unusual amount of aptitude and concentration, I shall ask Miss Fogelsang to be my partner in the act. Miss Fogelsang will shortly walk among the tables, asking if she may borrow some personal belongings from the audience, while I shall remain here on the stage. If you will please be silent while my partner concentrates, I shall attempt to receive her thoughts as they describe those belongings that you have temporarily entrusted to her. Is that fair enough?" Fontini paused.

A man in the audience asked if Fontini would be blindfolded.

"Ah, I forgot to mention that," replied Fontini, taking a black cloth from one of his pockets. "Yes, indeed, sir. I wonder if you would come up on the stage and help me tie this cloth over my eyes?"

The man joined Fontini. He examined the cloth to make sure that he could not see through it, folded it several times and tied it snugly around Fontini's head, so that the eyes were covered.

"Are you now convinced that there is no possible way I can see Miss Fogelsang?" asked Fontini.

The man once more inspected the position of the blindfolding cloth and said that he was satisfied.

"Thank you, sir. To make extra sure that I can't see anything, I shall, with your permission, remain here with my back turned to the audience. Miss Fogelsang, would you please collect the first object?"

The assistant stepped down from the stage. Among the numerous objects she was offered, she took a ring from a well-dressed lady. She inspected it and asked for silence while she concentrated.

After a brief pause, Señor Fontini pronounced, "Miss Fogelsang holds in her left hand a ring belonging to a lady. It is a clear diamond solitaire of approximately two and a half carats weight. And very beautiful, I might add."

After the applause, the assistant walked to another table, where a man handed her a heavy cigarette case. Fontini spoke again moments after the audience had become quiet. "Miss Fogelsang now holds a heavy cigarette case, made from silver, I believe, containing eleven Player's cigarettes of regular size. There is an inscription on the lid: '*Pour Emile, avec tout mon amour. Marie.*'"

The audience laughed and applauded loudly, as the owner counted the cigarettes and confirmed that Fontini was absolutely right in all he had quoted.

While several other articles were handed to the assistant, Bobby leaned over to Ann, whispering, "What an extraordinary ability. There are times when I wish that I could do something like that."

Ann looked teasingly at him. "You probably already have that ability, except that you are not conscious of it."

* * *

As the enthusiastic applause subsided at the conclusion of the scheduled program, and after both Señor Fontini and Miss Fogelsang had taken numerous bows for the satisfied audience, Señor Fontini held up his hands asking for silence. He looked professorially at the crowd.

"Ladies and gentlemen," he finally began. "You have been a wonderful audience, most kind and appreciative, as you have always been here in the Terrace Room. Miss Fogelsang and I thank you very much. In return we would like to add an unscheduled debut, never before shown on a stage anywhere in the world. Miss Fogelsang and I have worked on this act for quite some time, and we believe that it is finally ready to be shown to the public. As I mentioned earlier, the art of our profession is generally not well understood. But let me assure you again that, like in any other craft, it is primarily a matter of understanding the mediums one is working with combined with training and lots of experience. There is absolutely no supernatural or even mystical elements involved. The demonstration we are about to make is in a hitherto unexplored field that we have chosen to call 'memory erasing.' Let me start with briefly explaining what is meant by memory erasing."

A whisper ran through the room as Fontini continued. "As an analogy, let us say that the average age of all persons present here is forty years. Some of you, younger people, may be slightly offended by this supposition, but please do not take it as a personal insult. And perhaps some of those over forty might be flattered by my estimate, and I admit that you are looking well tonight and easily could pass for forty. However, that is not the point I wish to make. The point is that each of us is equipped with a mental faculty called a 'memory' that is continuously being imprinted, throughout our entire conscious life, with whatever each of us happen to experience through our senses. By analogy, you may say that our memories work pretty much in the same way as the common variety of video cassette recorders, also called VCRs. You probably already know that an operating VCR records sounds and images on the magnetic coating of a continuously moving tape, which can be played back later. If we say that the tape is running at three inches per second, which I am told is the minimum speed required to obtain a reasonable quality of the recording, the average forty-year-old person would have been recording for about three hundred fifty thousand hours. That comes to an equivalent total length of sixty thousand miles of recorded tape, about the same as two and a half times the circumference of the earth at equator. Be glad that your creator provided you with all that memory capacity free of charge. If you were to purchase the equivalent amount of magnetic tape to be able to remember your past, it would cost a small fortune! Perhaps some of us would not be able to afford memorizing all that took place for more than a few years.

"Now, on that imaginary tape in one's mind is recorded everything one has experienced during one's life. Not only what one has seen and heard, but also what has been felt, smelled, tasted, or imagined—trillions of impressions! Consequently these recordings, of course, supplemented by one's physical body and the remainder of the brain, determine who each of us is as an individual. They are influential in how we react to any given situation, our moods, or what we accept or reject. They impact our desires, fears, likes and dislikes, convictions or doubts, all our future thinking. This memory tape is literally one's main reference point or compass for future decisions, actions, and feelings.

"As previously mentioned, tonight is the first time we are demonstrating our new procedure for erasing selected clusters of memory in a person in full view of a large audience. During our research, we did encounter many practical difficulties in developing a reliable method, and I beg your indulgence if the experiment does not turn out to be 100 percent successful. I do assure you, however, that it is harmless to the medium, even if I obviously should be much chagrined if it failed. *C'est la vie*, as a philosophical Frenchman would claim. Again, please cooperate by not creating distractions during the trance, and I think that we should have a very good probability of success.

"The object of tonight's demonstration is therefore selective memory erasing, which, of course, is the opposite of memory reinforcing and quite different from posthypnotic suggestion, which I believe many of you are familiar with. I do not pretend that I can erase sixty thousand miles of tape in a few minutes. Fortunately, that is not humanly possible. I shall limit myself to let the audience select three well-known facts, such as the birthday of a well-known public person, the name of a famous college or landmark, the title of a song, to mention just a few. We shall then see if I can make the medium forget those three pieces of common knowledge.

"Let me emphasize that if I am successful in doing so, I shall fully restore the memory of those three pieces of knowledge at the end of experiment. And, as I have said, there will be no permanent loss of memory or other undesirable aftereffects. You may have complete confidence in me." Señor Fontini looked around the attentive audience as his assistant moved closer to him.

"And now," he continued, "I shall need a volunteer from the audience to participate in the experiment. I wonder if we have in our midst a courageous person who is willing to be tested? Perhaps even one, who is known among his or her family or friends for having a good memory. Incidentally, to make the outcome even more challenging, we have decided to offer a prize consisting of a bottle of Amontillado, the best the establishment can provide, if that volunteer can recall even one of the three pieces of knowledge we select for the experiment. Please, ladies and gentlemen?"

A murmur ran through the room. Helen looked at Stafford. "Didn't you mention that your mother has an amazing memory? Do you think that she may be willing to try it?"

Stafford turned towards his mother and asked, "Why not? Are you game, Mother?"

Ann McClure smiled and quickly replied, "Would I like to make a fool of myself? Yes, of course I would."

Stafford rose and spoke loudly, just as several other people were preparing to get up. "Mr. Fontini. May I nominate the lady with the best steel-trap memory in the western hemisphere, my mother, Ann McClure." The audience cheered approvingly.

Fontini looked delighted as his assistant stepped down from the stage and came to the McClures' table. He asked, "I do hope that Mrs. McClure accepts?"

Ann went up on the stage escorted by the assistant under scattered applause. Fontini took her hand and looked at the audience. "We are most fortunate to have a medium who not only is reputed to have a splendid memory, but also is a beautiful and charming lady. I bet you are a recent bride, Mrs. McClure?"

Ann could not help laughing. "Yes," she said. "Exactly twenty-five years ago."

"Today is your silver wedding anniversary? Congratulations to both you and your husband are in order."

Fontini nodded towards Bobby McClure at the table, and again, a polite applause broke out. "In that case, I do hope that you will win the Amontillado to help you celebrate. Now, Mrs. McClure, please relax. You are in good company, and your family is keeping an eye on us to make certain that everything is proper."

He then turned towards the audience. "As I outlined before, we now need three specific facts of which Mrs. McClure has firm knowledge. I invite suggestions."

A male voice in the background of the room called out, "What is your telephone number?" The audience chuckled.

Señor Fontini also laughed but answered disarmingly, "We better pass on that one. Can't we come up with some facts that are generally known?"

Another voice in the audience suggested, "What is the name of the English monarch?"

"Very good," said Señor Fontini. "Mrs. McClure, what is your memory?"

"Elizabeth II," she answered without hesitation.

"And right you are." That will be the first correct answer. Can we have another suggestion?"

A lady at one of the front tables spoke up. "What do the bells of St. Clement's say?"

Señor Fontini looked a little concerned. "If I am not mistaken, Mrs. McClure is from abroad, probably from North America? Do you know that nursery rhyme?" he asked Ann.

"The bells of St. Clement's?" She thought for a moment and then recited, "Oranges and lemons, say the bells of St. Clement's."

"Bravo. Excellent! So the correct answer is 'Oranges and lemons,'" mused Fontini. "Splendid imagination, thank you, my lady. And now for one final fact?"

Stafford again stood up and asked his mother, "What landmark did we visit today between two and three in the afternoon?"

"That was when we toured the Tower of London, as I recall," answered Ann.

"Is that true?" inquired Fontini, looking at Stafford.

"It is."

"Very well. Let's make the Tower of London the third correct answer." Fontini faced the audience.

"Ladies and gentlemen, as you heard, we have now selected three particular names or quotes of which Mrs. McClure has confirmed knowledge. I shall now, with Mrs. McClure's permission, try to erase that part of her memory which contains the answers we have agreed upon. If, after doing so, Mrs. McClure can recall even a single of the answers correctly, I owe her a bottle of fine Amontillado. And please refrain from helping Mrs. McClure by suggesting or whispering the answers. That wouldn't be fair to the experiment, would it? Mrs. McClure, please place yourself in the chair next to my assistant and make yourself comfortable. I promise to restore your memory completely if I am lucky enough to succeed in the experiment. Please relax and trust me. Will the audience please be quiet for a moment."

Ann sat down in the chair, crossed her legs, letting her hands rest in her lap, leaned back, and appeared to enjoy the moment. Señor Fontini stepped in front of her and established eye contact. He was very relaxed himself and spoke slowly in a soothing yet friendly monotone. "Please relax as much as you can, Mrs. McClure . . . The chair you are sitting in is very comfortable . . . Everything is in order . . . Relax. You are beginning to feel drowsy . . . Your eyelids feel heavy . . . very heavy . . . Everything is all right and you are completely relaxed . . . Yes, you may close your eyes. You do not hear anything except my voice. You feel pleasantly warm and comfortable and you are completely at ease."

The audience was hushed, and their attention riveted on Señor Fontini and Mrs. McClure. They saw Mrs. McClure's eyelids closing slowly, and her head nodded forward.

"Mrs. McClure, do you hear me?" asked Fontini.

"Yes," was the quiet reply from Ann.

"Mrs. McClure," continued Fontini in the same tone of voice. "You have often heard the name of the present English monarch. Would you please go back in your memory, and wherever you find the name of that monarch, tell yourself that you wish to expel it as if you had never heard of that name. The name will leave your memory, but I shall later restore it to exactly the same as it was before. But for now, that name is nowhere to be found in your memory.

"You have also heard of an old nursery rhyme about what the bells of St. Clement's is supposed to say. Please tell yourself that you wish to expel the explanation of what those bells are saying, as if you had never heard of it. The answer no longer exists in your memory. You know about the bells of St. Clement's, but for now, you have no memory of what the bells are saying in particular.

"And finally, Mrs. McClure, today you visited several places together with your family. Between two and three o'clock in the afternoon, you visited a famous structure or landmark, the name of which is presently in your memory. Please ask yourself to expel that name from your memory, as if you had never heard of it. You know the appearance and the location of that landmark, but presently you have no memory of its name. Thank you.

"Mrs. McClure, you are still completely relaxed. The items I mentioned have now been erased from your memory, as if you have never heard of them. In a few seconds I shall clap my hands, you will open your eyes and feel wonderfully refreshed and at ease."

Fontini took a step backward and counted "One, two, three," whereupon he clapped his hands lightly.

Ann opened her eyes and smiled. "How do you feel?" asked Fontini.

"I never felt better," replied Ann.

"Good. I hope that you remember that we started a little contest? If you can give the proper answer to any of three questions asked by the audience you will have won a bottle of Amontillado to help you celebrate your silver wedding anniversary. Right? If you will follow me, we shall begin the questioning." He took her arm and led her to the front of the stage facing the expectant audience.

Addressing the crowded room Señor Fontini continued, "I first want to apologize to the fine gentleman who proposed the question about Mrs. McClure's telephone number. I hope that he will understand my reasons for not accepting this particular proposal, and that he will forgive us for not using it. Now, will the other gentleman who asked the first question please repeat it?"

The voice from the audience asked again, "What is the name of the present English monarch?"

"Do you know the answer to that question, Mrs. McClure?" queried Fontini.

Ann thought for a moment. "I know that the monarch is a queen . . . I have seen pictures of her many times. Hmm . . . is it Mary? I am not sure."

The audience gasped in disbelief.

Señor Fontini looked kindly at her and said, "I am afraid not. Her majesty's name is Elizabeth II, and from now on, you will be able to remember her name distinctly. But do not worry, you have two more chances to win. Will the lady at the front table please repeat the second question?" He pointed at the table.

"What do the bells of St. Clement's say?"

Ann thought again. She looked obviously bewildered. "I have heard of a church named St. Clement's, but what can bells say other than 'ding dong?'"

Fontini held a hand lightly around Ann's shoulders. "Mrs. McClure, there is an old nursery rhyme that goes like this:

'Oranges and lemons, say the bells of St. Clement's.'

"'Oranges and lemons' would have been the correct answer. You will, from now on, remember that rhyme with distinction too. But, do not give up yet. You have tried valiantly, and we have yet one question to go. Will the younger McClure please state the third question?"

Stafford rose and asked his mother, "What landmark did we visit today between two and three p.m.?"

Ann looked searchingly at Stafford. "We went on a bus tour and stopped at a large castle or fortress at about that time. We walked in and saw a great number of uniforms and weapons on display. I also remember the torture chambers. Its name is probably well known, but it escapes me at this moment. Was it Madame

Tussaud?—No, that was a wax museum . . . so many names to remember! Goodness, this is ridiculous! I cannot think of that name. I know that it is right on the Thames River."

Señor Fontini looked sympathetically at her and asked, "Do you then give up?"

"Yes, I don't seem to be able to come up with a name for that landmark other than it was a fortress."

"Well. That fortress is named 'The Tower of London.' You will remember that name easily in the future. 'The Tower of London' would have been the correct answer. But let me assure you that you do have an excellent memory, and that I for a moment was afraid that I would not be able to complete the experiment successfully."

After the applause, Señor Fontini took Ann's arm and asked, addressed to the crowd, "Don't you agree with me that Mrs. McClure is an excellent sport and deserves a reward for her courage and charm?"

"Hear, hear" was heard from the room, and applause broke out again.

Fontini turned to Ann and said, "Mrs. McClure, it has been a real pleasure to work with you, and I appreciate your willingness to participate in our show. I shall personally make sure that a bottle of the best Amontillado the house can provide is brought to your table in a little while. And now, please let my assistant escort you back to your table."

Señor Fontini finished his show, thanking all participants and the whole audience once again for their cooperation and enthusiasm, and he and his assistant received a standing ovation.

* * *

Chapter 4

A Bottle of Amontillado

When Ann returned to the McClure's table, she laughed and asked Stafford, "Did I not make a complete fool of myself?"

"No. You did beautifully, Mother. We are proud of you. Anyway, who can stand up to a wizard? No one could have done any better than you did."

Helen was curious and asked, "How does it feel to be hypnotized?"

"I don't remember feeling anything unusual. It was just like having a normal conversation like we are having now. Fontini has a marvelous ability to make one feel at ease. I think that he is a very sympathetic person," replied Ann.

"I hope that you did not learn anything that you are going to try out on me," interjected her husband with a contrived frown.

"Oh, come on, Bobby." Ann laid her hands on one of Bobby's. "Have I not put up with you for twenty-five years so far? I can take it a little longer."

The stage became busy again as the band returned and arranged themselves. They opened up with a smooth fox trot, and several couples went to the dance floor. Stafford and Helen joined the dancers.

"Do you remember when we were their age?" asked Ann, halfway to Bobby and halfway to herself. "Life was so simple and beautiful. No responsibilities, or at least relatively few. We were looking ahead to the future with confidence. Nothing could go wrong, we thought. And it has worked out well! We have good memories, sweet memories, isn't that a wonderful thing to have? We truly have been blessed, Bobby, don't you think? And I pray that Stafford and Helen will be happy together too! Do you know what, Bobby? I still love you as much as I did then!"

"I love you too, Ann, more than words can say," Bobby said, and took her hand in his. "Yes, we have been very fortunate. I still cannot believe that our wedding was twenty-five years ago. I remember the day as if it were yesterday . . . a beautiful spring day. The shrubs and flowers on the hillsides were in full bloom. Do you remember that I had forgotten where I put your wedding band when the minister asked for it in front of everybody? I finally found it in my hip pocket, but it must have taken an eternity before I did. At least that's the way I felt. How careless of me!" He chuckled at the thought. "And on the way to our honeymoon in Pensacola one of the front tires in my old Plymouth blew out, and the spare tire was flat too. I had to leave you alone in the car for more than an hour, while I took the spare to the nearest service station." He chuckled again. "Yes, it seems funny now, but at the time I felt miserable. You must have thought that I was a complete oaf? But it has been good times. All twenty-five years have been good times."

"Yes, I remember it all very well, Bobby. And I never thought of you as an oaf. On the contrary, you are, and have always been, a fine man. Do you remember when . . ." The couple kept talking tenderly of many shared events from their past.

The band finished the tune and began a new one, and then one more. The moment was pregnant with memories for Bobby and Ann, as if a treasure chest had been opened in front of their eyes. "Do you remember when . . . ? See here . . . What did you think of that?"

* * *

Stafford and Helen were both excellent dancers. They had first met in a square-dancing circle and had later taken classes in ballroom dancing together. Tonight, however, they avoided the elegant and complicated steps and danced very basic steps close to each other, cheek to cheek. The smooth rhythms carried them slowly around the dance floor. It was obvious to anyone watching them that they were in love.

They did not stop dancing until the band leader announced a short intermission, and they returned to the table.

The four were engaged in a discussion about how to spend the next day, when Señor Fontini and his assistant showed up at their table. Señor Fontini had changed into a basic dark business suit, blue shirt, and a striped tie. His assistant wore a knee length subdued evening dress in blue and gray and jewelry to match. Señor Fontini carried a tray with an uncorked bottle and six sherry glasses on it.

"Hello, Mrs. McClure. We thought that we would personally make sure that you received your hard-won prize," said Fontini with an easy smile, as he placed the tray on the table. "Are you enjoying yourselves?"

Ann rose and touched his sleeve lightly. "How thoughtful of you, Señor Fontini. Thank you. I hope that you can join us for a little while? We were all captivated by your show." Ann went on to introduce her family, and Fontini introduced his assistant as his wife of fourteen years. Her first name was Gretchen, and she appeared to be about fifteen years younger than her husband.

After they had sat down, Fontini placed a glass in front of each and filled them from the bottle. "I do hope that you enjoy a good sherry? I hasten to add that I did *not* make this bottle myself! May I propose a toast for the silver anniversary couple? May the best years of your marriage yet be ahead," he said, as he lifted his glass. "Congratulations, Mr. and Mrs. McClure."

Having tasted the sherry, Bobby put down his glass and replied, "Thank you very much. Ann and I do appreciate your kind wishes." Addressed to Señor Fontini, he added, "I am not much of an expert on sherries, but this one tastes delicious. And let me honestly tell you that your show is first class too. I would go as far as to say that it is the most interesting I have attended. Good entertainment, unique and a real eye opener. I simply can't remember ever having been as absorbed in what I saw on a stage. Tell us, if you don't mind, how you happened to become an illusionist?"

Fontini stroked his forehead several times before he answered, "It is quite a long and twisted story. But if you will indulge me, I shall gladly try to answer you. My particular field is very much a specialty niche in the entertainment world. There are no schools or handbooks in the Western world that teaches how to become a genuine illusionist, except maybe in the field of magic tricks, which, as you probably know, is basically a matter of dexterity, flair, and having the proper equipment. No, in my field, you must naturally have or laborously acquire a unique blend of certain types of knowledge, intuition, showmanship, and people rapport. Generally, those who are the best in the trade are reluctant to discuss their methodology with anyone else, as it potentially could detract from their performances.

"I think that I first became interested in becoming an illusionist in my early childhood. Our family often went to circuses, where I was particularly enthralled by the magician shows. I also remember going to theaters and shows with my parents to see well-known magicians, hypnotists, telepathists, and so on. In retrospect, most of them were not very original, and you can still see the same acts performed all over the world today.

"My father also inspired me, probably unintentionally. He was a teacher in history and philosophy in the 'gymnasium' in Innsbruck, Austria. Mind you that a gymnasium in Austria is a preparatory school for students who intend to enter a university. He was an outstanding teacher, I think, and we often spent hours together discussing history and philosophy. The classical Greeks were his favorite subject. For some years, my ambition actually was to become a professor, teaching philosophy and psychology.

"As a hobby, I had taught myself several magical tricks beginning when I was about eleven or twelve years old. Card tricks, alternatively disappearing and reappearing objects, interlocking rings being taken apart or rearranged, that sort of things! Much to my surprise, I found that many people in Innsbruck were willing to pay me for entertaining their children at birthday parties. I invested my earnings in more equipment and developed more acts. By the time I was eighteen, I had a considerable reputation in Innsbruck as an illusionist and magician. Back in those days, I was performing under my birth name of 'Hans Schneider.'

"I then entered the University in Vienna, but I did not do very well from the start, probably because of my preoccupation with the magician shows, which I continued to offer. At the end of my second year at the university, I was drafted into military service. When the war ended in 1945, conditions were very bad in Austria. However, I was fortunate enough to land a small job at a well-known night club in Vienna, giving two performances every evening.

"After the show one night, I was surprised to be sought out by a gentleman who introduced himself as Giovanni Montebiera, one of the best-known magicians and illusionists in Europe at that time. I had met him in Italy about eighteen months earlier, when he performed in a show for military personnel. Somehow, I must have made an impression on him. To make a long story short, he had come to watch my act and apparently thought well of it. He told me that he was looking for a younger partner and if I would consider joining him. I was, of course, honored and elated, and I accepted on the spot.

"I never regretted that. Montebiera was one of the nicest and most caring human beings I have ever met, and a brilliant teacher as well. We traveled together for twelve years in Europe, Africa, and the Americas. Montebiera is, of course, Italian, so I started billing myself under the name of Fontini. Montebiera died suddenly from a stroke after a performance in Genoa in 1958. It was a great personal loss for me. I loved and respected him as if he had been my own father or brother. He was a true master in his field, and he, far more than anyone else, taught me what I know about the intricacies of my trade." Fontini's face had become somber, while he talked about his late friend and mentor.

Helen interjected, "Montebiera must have been a great man, I mean both professionally and as a human being. I do wish that I could have met with him. Señor Fontini, or shall I say Mr. Schneider, don't you think that on the average there were more people like Mr. Montebiera when you were my age? What I intend to say is this: It seems to me that people in general are becoming less caring and more violent in our time. Nowadays, one watches and reads so much about crime and violence and war!"

"A good question, my young lady," replied Fontini. "We all know that the statistics for crime in most so-called civilized countries have gotten worse, and that military and political conflicts abound all over the world. I tend to believe, though, that it is mostly our sensitivity to these problems that has increased, largely because of more intense news coverage. When I was young, I still remember reading in the newspapers about wars in Spain, Ethiopia, and China. In addition, I, firsthand, lived through the Second World War. I also read about murders and other crimes in Austria and elsewhere. But we did not have television to show us all the gory details, and not too many people had radios before the midthirties. But I certainly agree with you that the world is badly in need of more individuals like Montebiera, and probably always has been."

Helen pressed her questioning, "A few years ago, I read about a case in New York City where a man was knifed on a street. He lay there bleeding for more than an hour crying to people walking by, 'Please help me,' before he finally died. Later, the police estimated that at least one hundred persons must have passed the wounded man, and not a single one cared enough to even call a doctor or an ambulance. That's really scary!"

Stafford broke in, "I read that story too. It was thought that people did not want to get involved, because they knew that there were gangs fighting each other in the area. I agree with Helen that it seems as if the Good Samaritan is a rapidly vanishing species, at least in many parts of the United States. Not only are there more crimes, but in general, people seem to care less about the victims."

Bobby changed the drift of the conversation by asking Fontini, "You are Austrian then? I understand that Austria is a beautiful country, full of mountains and music, just like where I come from. I assume that you both enjoy your mountains?"

"If we do? We miss them every day we don't see them. Mountains somehow give one a feeling of serenity, an unexplainable peace in the soul. Of *stimmung*, as we say in Austria. The closest English translation I know of stimmung is 'mood,' although that doesn't express it very accurately. Isn't that the way you feel about it, Schatz?" Fontini looked at his wife.

Gretchen's English was slightly less fluid than Mr. Fontini's, and her accent quite a bit more distinct. She answered, "Yes, we both love to be in the mountains, it is so much nicer. We have a house in the mountains just outside Solbad Hall in Austria, with an open, beautiful view over the Inn River valley. We try to stay there at least three months every summer and two months in the winter. Hans and I plan to go back when our London contract expires by the end of this month. Yes, we do feel very much at home in just about any mountains, and we go mountain hiking whenever our travel plans permit it. Where did you say you live?"

Replied Ann, "We live near the town of Boone in North Carolina. It's in the Appalachian Mountains in the eastern part of the United States of America. The Great Smokies National Park is about sevetny-five miles to the southwest. Have you been there?"

"Yes, I think so," said Gretchen, searching her memory. "We had a tour in the United States about ten years ago, or thereabouts. There were a few free days between shows in Atlanta, Georgia and Washington, DC, so we rented a car and drove leisurely up through the mountains. We even did a little bit of mountain hiking, as I remember it. Yes, I also remember the breathtaking views from the Blue Ridge Parkway. We must do that again, nicht wahr, Hans?"

"If you do," interjected Ann, "be sure to come and visit with us. Just ask for Bobby McClure in Boone. It would be so nice to meet with you again, and you are welcome to stay with us if you like."

Gretchen took a small book from her purse and made a note in it. "Thank you, Mrs. McClure, we should like to do that very much. What kind of business is your husband in?"

Ann laughed, "I don't know if you would call it a business. Bobby is the sheriff of Boone County, now serving for his fourth term. I suppose that you could call him a politician. We also own a small nursery, but that is mainly my responsibility, at least for the time being."

Bobby explained, "The nursery started as a hobby after Stafford began attending school. We both love horticulture, especially Ann. It is such a good way to relax. Each year seems to be better for business than the last, and we now employ three part-time helpers. Hopefully Ann will be able to take care of me after I retire from politics," he said with a big smile and jabbing Ann lightly.

"County sheriff? Isn't that the same as 'Gauleiter,' Hans?" asked Gretchen.

"I think that there is a lot of similarity," replied her husband.

"Our department is mainly responsible for public safety, enforcement of law and order, and bringing to justice individuals suspected of violations. We have several other duties too, but those are the most important," explained Bobby.

The band had returned and resumed playing, this time a slow waltz. Stafford and Helen looked at each other and asked to be excused. They left for the dance floor.

Mr. Fontini filled the glasses once more, and they sipped the Amontillado. "So you are here on a vacation then?" You chose a good time. England is the loveliest in June. Do you have any particular plans for your stay here?"

Ann replied, "We normally don't travel a great deal, certainly not, compared to you. This is the first time we are outside of our own country, so you can see that we are not exactly world travelers. However, Bobby has, for many years, wanted to visit Scotland, from where his grandparents emigrated. We don't have contacts with any relatives in Scotland, but we hope to stumble into a few of them. That would be really interesting. We are leaving London the day after tomorrow."

Bobby added, "It's some kind of nostalgia I have. There are a great many families of Scottish ancestry in our area. They all seem to revere the old country. I simply had to find out for myself what they were talking about, I suppose. So Ann and I decided to give ourselves a two-week vacation over here as an anniversary gift. We just arrived this morning."

The band was now playing the gentle melody of "Edelweiss," the well-known song about the small flower commonly found in the Alps. Gretchen began humming the tune, and her husband joined her, linking arms and swaying in time to the music. Ann and Bobby joined in the humming. Gretchen finished by singing out, "Edelweis, Edelweis, bleibst du ewig mein Schatz."

"That was very beautiful," exclaimed Ann as the music ended. "I feel so good tonight. I wish that it could last forever."

Gretchen prodded Bobby McClure, "It must be an exciting occupation to be the county sheriff."

"I do enjoy my department. We have a staff of excellent people—good people. The population in Boone County are mostly fine people too, and we have a splendid relationship. Yes, I like my job," Bobby replied modestly.

"So you don't have the problem of increasing crime and violence that Helen spoke of earlier?" Gretchen inquired.

Bobby stroked a hand through his burly hair and reflected pensively, his lips pursed. After a couple of seconds he replied, "Ordinarily not, I am glad to say. Most of our caseloads are traffic tickets, some few burglaries, and occasionally traffic accidents. Once in a while, we are called to settle a domestic discord. Most of them are handled routinely. Incidents of violence do occur though, but they are rare events, fortunately. But once in a while, events happen that makes my job pretty exciting!"

"I am sure that when it happens you always catch and punish the criminals, just like the sheriffs do in the American movies?" cajoled Gretchen with a mischievous smile.

Bobby could not help laughing at Gretchen's allegory. "I am afraid that you Europeans have a somewhat outdated picture of today's American law enforcement. No, we don't have any citizens' posses in our county, and the department does not own a single horse. We do have professional detectives and investigators, as well as trained deputies. And, yes, in the vast majority of cases, we do manage to solve the crimes and catch and prosecute those responsible."

"You cannot mean not always?" asked Gretchen with a touch of disappointment in her tone of voice.

Bobby McClure emptied the remaining Amontillado from his glass and filled the glasses once more from the sherry bottle. "Yes, I must confess that, strictly speaking, we do have a few unsolved cases in our files. Those are the cases where all available clues led to dead ends, or perhaps only were presumed to be clues and did not fit anywhere. Or there may have been no survivors or witnesses to explain what took place. Occasionally, it also happens that witnesses, for some reason or another, withhold testimonies and evidences, or even falsify their statements. If you are interested, let me mention a particular case that caused a lot of headaches for us?" He awaited the response.

"I would like to hear that very much," replied Gretchen. Her husband nodded.

Ann interrupted disarmingly. "Really, you must excuse Bobby! He simply cannot get his work out of his mind. Is it one I have heard of before, Bobby?"

"You may have heard bits and pieces of it, but probably not the whole affair, Ann."

"Please let us hear it, Sheriff! I am all ears! I simply adore detective novels. What say they? I am nuts about them!" goaded Gretchen with a laugh.

* * *

Chapter 5

Case of the Four Motorcyclists

Bobby McClure began explaining: "In early June of 1975, two of our young highway patrolmen left the headquarters' garage at about eight thirty in the morning in a regularly marked patrol car. The driver was Lonnie Ipsen. In the passenger's seat was Robert Tatum. I knew them both personally as well-liked and disciplined deputies, who, at that time, had been with the department for respectively eight years and a year and a half. They were both married and had young children.

"Their assignment was routine patrol of state road Route 105 between Jonas Ridge and Boone, a distance of about twenty miles. Route 105 is a two-lane winding highway in very hilly terrain, which is normally carrying a heavy traffic load, especially in the vacation season which was just beginning. Passing is difficult on Route 105 due to the many hilltops and curves, and it has narrow shoulders in most places, making parking of broken-down vehicles a potential hazard. Route105 parallels the Blue Ridge Parkway, which, at that time, was under construction in the nearby Grandfather Mountain area, and it was therefore being used as a detour for parkway traffic.

"Having reached Jonas Ridge without incidents, the patrol car turned back and parked after a curve outside of Pineville. The deputies were watching for speeding vehicles and other traffic violators. At about nine thirty, they observed four northbound motorcycles occupying both lanes coming around the curve and thus endangering a southbound car. The speed of the motorcycles was estimated to be in excess of sixty miles per hour, whereas the posted speed limit in the curve is forty miles per hour. Ipsen and Tatum gave chase immediately with the blue lights flashing."

* * *

At the point of his narration, where he arrived at the scene of the wrecked Q2 and saw the ambulance personnel placing a stretcher under the bleeding and unconscious Ipsen, Bobby McClure made a pause. It was obvious that the event had left a deep impression with him. He took a sip from his glass, as if to clear his throat.

Mr. Fontini broke the interlude by commenting, "I am afraid that most of the public do not appreciate the occupational hazards for personnel in the law-enforcing agencies who are so dedicated to protecting them. Did Ipsen and Tatum recover?"

"Well," replied McClure. "Tatum recovered quickly. Other than bruises and relatively minor cuts, he suffered a broken collar bone and a hairline fracture of the bone of the right upper arm. He was back on restricted duty after a week, and the cast was removed after four weeks. He never complained. Ipsen had a tough time though. We transferred him the same day to the medical center in Charlotte. He had a severe concussion, spinal compression, numerous cuts in the face and on the upper torso, and glass splinters in both eyes. The doctors did their best, and he was released in a wheelchair two weeks later. Still later, he went back for a cornea transplant. Even so, his eyesight on the right eye is down to 50 percent. Worst of all is that he still suffers from periodic dizziness at which times he is unable to focus his eyes. His wife also tells me that sometimes he wakes up with nightmares, holding his eyes for minutes before she can calm him down."

Looking at Mr. Fontini, Ann asked, "I wonder if it would be possible to help Ipsen by erasing this incident from his memory, in the same way as you did it with me in your show?"

Mr. Fontini pursed his lips and thought for a moment. "I am afraid that it is impossible to predict the outcome in Ipsen's case," he answered at last. "First of all, such a procedure is not practiced by the medical profession to the best of my knowledge. But more important, Ipsen may have suffered irreversible neurological injuries, which may be the main cause of his spells. And finally, a long time has elapsed since the incident. It may be impossible to reconstruct his traumas with precision. It is an interesting idea though!"

McClure sighed, "I wish that someone could help Ipsen. He deserves it."

Gretchen looked again at Bobby McClure and asked, "And the motorcyclists? Did you apprehend them?"

"As a matter of fact we did, but not in the way you would expect. Let's get to that." McClure stroked his eyes.

* * *

McClure continued describing the hunt for the four motorcyclists ending with their dead bodies being discovered three days later at the base of the Watauga Overlook bluff. When the sheriff made a pause, Gretchen shrugged her shoulders and concluded, "Based on what you have told us, it seems to me that you did finish the job. Is there any doubt in your mind that they were the persons responsible for the wreck of the police car and the injuries to Ipsen and Tatum?"

"None whatsoever," answered McClure. "The fingerprints on the bottle fragments matched those of one of the dead men, the biggest of them. We also found fingerprints on the motorcycles, which exactly matched those of the four men. And finally, Tatum testified that the dress and general appearance of the motorcyclists, as well as the motorcycles themselves, were identical to what he had observed during the pursuit.

"We were also able to assemble psychological profiles of the four. The man who threw the bottle was known among his comrades as 'High Command.' He had two records of assault, one against a foreman in a company he had worked for and the other in a street mugging. He had spent times in jail in New Jersey at both occasions. The one who was found with a knife in the back was apparently nicknamed 'SS' and had served a jail sentence for assault and sex offense. We also found out that only three weeks earlier, he had been charged with rape outside of St. Petersburg, Florida, but that the plaintiff had withdrawn her accusation a few days later. The last two, known as 'Firebird' and 'Crazy,' had been mutual friends since childhood. They both had records of petty burglary, muggings, and disorderly conduct. If history is any guide, and it usually is, those individuals would have been the perfect suspects."

Gretchen looked puzzled. "So what questions remain to be answered to make sure that justice was done?"

McClure scratched his neck. "Well, the circumstances of the motorcyclist's deaths are murky, to say the least. In the absence of witnesses, how was it possible to construct a reasonable sequence of events where all four somehow ended up dead, left in an inaccessible area below the overlook? I mentioned that SS was killed by a knife in his back, which incidentally belonged to himself! Who did it and why? Based on the location of his body, it appears that he was forcibly pushed or thrown from the overlook. From the bruises on High Command's body, it would appear that he had been badly beaten while still alive. How did that come about, considering that he was a big and powerful man? Same questions. Firebird's body had fresh second and third degree burns on the neck, shoulders and back. How did that happen? The cause of his death was actually a broken neck, probably a result of falling from the overlook. The last one, Crazy, was apparently the only one who had not been injured before he went over the cliff at about the same place Firebird did. That fall could have been accidental as his blood alcohol level was sky high. As you can see, Mrs. Schneider, there are plenty of questions we don't have answers for."

His listeners sat in silence as if waiting to hear the solution. At length, McClure continued, "Of course, we combed the overlook and the surrounding areas for clues. Unfortunately, that was three days after the incident, and heavy rains had, in the meantime, washed and scrambled everything on the ground. Apart from the four rider's jackets, we found fragments of bottles, some pop drink and beer cans, and a knife belonging to High Command in the thicket below the bluff. The fingerprints on the knife were his own. There were several faint blood stains on the overlook, approximately in line with the location of High Command's body. Laboratory analyses of the stains were inconclusive. We also found scraps of paper and plastic film, a few coins, several pieces of rope, and two unidentified buttons, to mention just a few of the items. The footprints we found were badly washed out. There were no freshly broken branches, trampled grass, and so on, which might be suggestive of a struggle having taken place.

"The coroner established the time of the death of the four men to within a few hours of each other and approximately forty-eight to seventy-two hours before the recovery of the bodies Friday afternoon. Thus they may have died on the day of the bottle-throwing incident or, at the latest, the next day, Wednesday. All four must have been drinking quite heavily, judged by the alcohol level in their blood and stomach.

"We tried to narrow down the time of their deaths by contacting the parties we knew had been on the mountain that Tuesday and Wednesday. The young couple, who came out at the Route 184 intersection at about half past four Tuesday afternoon was finally traced to Winston-Salem. An insurance salesman, as I recall. He told that he and his girlfriend had started very early and had spent some time on the Watauga Overlook, leaving there at about half past ten, heading for Grandfather Mountain. They did not use the fireplace, and there was no fire in it when they left. Two other visitors appeared on the overlook while they were there. At any rate, the motorcyclists could not have arrived on the overlook that early, as it must have been past ten before they had parked and camouflaged their motorcycles in the woods more than two miles away.

"The group of Boy Scouts exiting from the northern trail at about five p.m. came from Boone and had spent the day hiking to the Watauga River, where they had stayed for several hours. The Scout leader told us that they had not been within three quarter of a mile of the overlook, and that they had neither seen nor heard anything out of the ordinary.

"The party of eight, which exited at about six p.m. Tuesday afternoon at the Route 184 intersection, was difficult to trace. We finally located the owner of one of the cars, a Mr. Henderson in Hickory, North Carolina, who owns a small plumbing contracting business. He said that they had arrived the same day at about nine a.m., together with their son and one of his friends plus another couple. They had hiked to the overlook, making some short stops on the way. They had used the fireplace to grill hot dogs and hamburgers. While they were on the overlook, they were joined by a middle-aged couple who introduced themselves as Mr. and Mrs. Taylor. The Henderson party and the Taylors left the overlook together a little after three in the afternoon, making a few stops on the way down. To the best of Henderson's recollection, the fireplace had not been rekindled by the time they left, and he was certain that the Taylors were the only ones they had met while they were on the overlook.

"We can therefore reasonably assume that the Taylors were the middle-aged couple the insurance salesman and his girlfriend had met earlier in the day. That leaves, among the persons we knew had been on the mountain Tuesday, only the two students from Charlotte. Unfortunately, we have no account of where and when they exited, but if, as Henderson explained, they were headed south on the upper trail, that means away from the overlook, at about four in the afternoon, it is most unlikely that they would have turned around and hiked back towards Watauga Overlook after their meeting. We tried, of course, to locate the two students at the higher educational institutions in Charlotte, and there are quite a few. However, no one stepped forward."

McClure took another sip from his glass before he continued. "As far as we know, only one group consisting of three young men from Banner Elk entered the mountain trails the following day, Wednesday. They started in the early afternoon but returned to the parking lot an hour and a half later. They explained to the waiting deputies that the trails were almost impassable. Surely, they could not have reached the overlook within that span of time.

"So the only logical conclusion is that the four motorcyclists must have been hiking unobserved through the woods beginning at some time after ten a.m., and arrived at the overlook sometime after three or perhaps half past three. They must have rekindled the fireplace, which by then must have been nearly burned out. One wonders why, considering that it was a mild and pleasant day, confirmed by the fact that they had taken their jackets off and that there was no utensils or food packaging to be found. Anyway, it started raining at about half past five, which must have extinguished the fire quite quickly. Because of the heavy rain during the night, followed by several showers Wednesday morning, it is unlikely that a new fire could have been started Wednesday from the available deadwood.

"We can therefore establish that Firebird somehow ended up on his back in the fireplace not later than, let us say, a quarter to six Tuesday. That would have been the only source of heat intensive enough to cause the extent of his burns. The wounds must have been excruciatingly painful, and we know that their group didn't carry any first-aid supplies. Firebird could possibly have jumped off the overlook in a blind desire to end his horrible sufferings. If so, the three others must have died before sunset the same day.

"Also, it seems strange that at least some of them didn't return to their motorcycles well before the rain began, if they had hoped to escape that same night, as the circumstances would indicate. They had taken no or only scant supplies with them, and their sleeping bags were still strapped to their motorcycles. Furthermore, there are no shelters in the vicinity of the overlook. Being experienced outdoor men, they must have noticed the coming change of weather and known that hiking in steep terrain in a heavy downpour, especially after dark, is nearly impossible. It would have been at least a two hours hike back to their motorcycles even in good light and dry weather. The fact that none of them had his jacket on when found would tend to support the view that all four probably had died before the rain started at about half past five.

"Our best estimate, based on known facts and the time it would take to warm up the fireplace again, is therefore that the events that led to the deaths of the four took place between the hours of half past three and half past five in the afternoon. Were anyone else present during that time span? We did not come up with any possibilities! And even if an unknown group of hikers, in spite of all odds, had encountered the motorcycle riders on the overlook, what motive could they have had to attack them? The riders carried hunting knives and were capable fighters. They certainly would have been formidable adversaries, and odds are that at least some of their attackers would have been seriously hurt, unless they perhaps were carrying guns. But there were no bullet wounds in the bodies or spent cartridges on the overlook!

"We also checked with nearby hospitals, but no persons had been treated for knife wounds or injuries associated with hand to hand fighting that whole week. Furthermore, both Crazy's and Firebird's corpses were found with their knives sheathed.

"So, you see, all available clues and pieces of information seemed to suggest that some kind of mutual quarrel must have broken out among the intoxicated motorcyclists after their arrival at the deserted overlook! In a very short span of time, they either killed each other, committed suicide, or had a fatal accident. We tried for months to come up with a more plausible hypothesis of what had happened.

"We therefore went back to Mr. Henderson to confirm that he had not inadvertently misquoted the time of his party's departure from the overlook on that day. He stuck to his previous explanation, which was confirmed by this wife and the other couple they had taken with them, who happened to live only a few houses down their street. Mr. and Mrs. Wannamaker, as I recall, both employed as teachers in the Hickory School District. All four agreed that their party had arrived shortly past noon, had used the fireplace for grilling their lunch, and had packed and left between three and three-thirty without having seen the motorcyclists or anyone else on the overlook except the Taylors. Asked if they were willing to testify under oath, they said 'yes' without reservation. They were unable to give any useful information about the Taylors, except that they thought that they might be Canadians from Montreal, and that they had enjoyed their company. Their cars separated shortly after they had left the parking lot. Without being absolutely certain, they all thought that the fireplace had pretty well burned out by the time they left."

* * *

Chapter 6

The Grand Jury's Investigation

"Absolutely fascinating! So what did you make out of it, Sheriff?" queried Fontini, raising his eyebrows. He took the bottle and poured the remaining Amontillado into the glasses.

"I remember reading about that case being presented before the grand jury," interjected Ann. "It must have been in the late fall of 1975, wasn't it, Bobby?"

"Right, Ann. Your memory always amazes me. The district court assembled the grand jury about four months after the incident. In two separate sessions, all events and circumstances, most of which I have already touched on, were reviewed in minute details. The hearings were reported by the local press but received only scant attention in the national news media. As often happens, when you don't have all the answers, strange rumors had begun to circulate in the county. One paper quoted, from a 'usually reliable source,' that the motorcyclists actually had been drug smugglers, and that they had been killed by the buyers as they handed over their merchandise. Another rumor, unfortunately, had it that friends of Ipsen and Tatum had organized a posse that did away with the four motorcyclists after they had been cornered on the overlook.

The rumors created lots of public attention and speculation, and the court hearings had record attendance.

"The judge was very deliberate, keeping all possibilities open. We finally convinced everyone present that no one else could have been present on the overlook at the time the four died. But, hard as we tried, we could not establish any motives, scenarios, or sequences of events other than the suggestion that Firebird, in his drunken stupor, might have stumbled into the fireplace and then jumped off the cliff to end the unbearable pain of his wounds. Based on the positions of the bodies, it might also have been possible that his old friend Crazy might have tried to prevent him from jumping, and was dragged or pushed off the overlook by Firebird in the ensuing shuffle. As to the deaths of the remaining two, we could not even make a wild guess."

Gretchen, who had listened to McClure's description with unusual interest, interrupted, "I think that I am beginning to understand what you meant when you said that some cases lead only to a dead end. What was the verdict of the jury?"

"The grand jury ruled that the four had died during an unexplainable private melee, and that no other persons had been involved in their deaths. Not a single one voiced disagreement with the verdict. That was a most unexpected outcome!"

"I agree that it may sound strange to us," added Fontini. "But if the jury came to that conclusion after all the work your department had done to solve the case, I don't think that there is anything else that I can add."

"I still think that there was something we overlooked or didn't think of. What really baffles me is the angle of that knife," exclaimed McClure, rubbing his chin.

"Now I am afraid that I don't follow you at all?" replied Gretchen.

"I was thinking of the position of the knife in SS's back. I believe that I mentioned that the murdering weapon was still stuck firmly in SS's corpse when we found it. It was obvious that the handle had received some blows, presumably from impacts as he fell or was pushed away from the overlook. Tell me, Mrs. Schneider, if someone decided to stab another person in the back, how would the knife be situated?"

"I would presume something like this," replied Gretchen, imitating an overhand thrust with her clenched hand, as if she had a knife in it.

"That's what I would think, usually. And depending on the relative position of the torsos of the assailant and the victim, the knife would enter higher or lower. As you probably know, a person's rib cage is much better protected against a deep knife wound than, for example, the abdominal area. Particularly when the knife is thrust into the back, where the shoulder blades will act as obstacles in addition to the ribs. But let's assume that you managed to aim the knife between the bone structures, Mrs. Fontini, what would be the direction of the knife's penetration?"

"The knife's blade would probably be slanting downwards. I mean that the tip of the blade would be lower than the point of entry in the back," replied Gretchen.

"Precisely!" exclaimed McClure. "But in SS's case, the knife blade was pointing upwards, between twenty or thirty degrees, and the blade was pretty much oriented sideways, meaning that the flat sides were pointing nearly straight up and down. Had it not been so, chances are that the knife would not have penetrated nearly as deep as it did. Rather than having entered as a result of an overhand thrust, I venture to say that the knife was slowly pressed or pushed in while SS was embracing his assailant, or perhaps while he was lying flat on his stomach. That would suggest that he must have been unaware of his assailant's intention to stab him, wouldn't you say?"

"That would seem to be a valid deduction," replied Gretchen, gazing curiously at McClure.

"We did not find any fingerprints on the knife's handle, which was smeared with SS's own blood. It would have been interesting to know which of the other three motorcyclists had last held it in his hand. I don't expect that it was High Command. From what we found out, he and SS had been close friends for too long. However, even that would be possible, I suppose. Crazy is an unlikely prospect too. He was physically the smallest of them, and from the information we gathered the least aggressive. By elimination, one would conclude that Firebird murdered SS. If so, what was his motivation, and why didn't he use his own knife which he had easy access to? Well, it is possible that Firebird could have lost his knife at that moment? Was there any connection between Firebird's burns and his use of SS's knife? Who knows? Did his burns occur before or after he stabbed SS? One can go on and on speculating." Bobby McClure stroked his neck while shaking his head.

"Yes, Sheriff, I have to agree with you. All the clues you have mentioned so far seem to lead only into the unknown, which you are most reluctant to accept!" replied Gretchen.

There was a pause in the conversation while everyone appeared lost in their own thoughts. McClure broke the interlude by suddenly raising his head with a resolute and excited expression on his face. "You know, I had not thought much about this case after the grand jury's investigation almost ten years ago. And I realize that I have already taken quite some time in recounting it for you. But upon reflection, as I was talking, I thought of some previously overlooked angles that could have affected our evaluation. By changing a few of the assumptions that were used, it may be possible to come up with a perfectly plausible chain of events leading up to what really took place on the overlook that day. However, were I to explain them, it would take even more of our time, and I certainly don't want to be a bore. I leave it to your discretion whether I should stop elaborating or if you want to hear more about this case."

"My dear sheriff," encouraged Gretchen, "when one lives in a hotel seven or eight months a year and is occupied for only two or three hours every day, life easily becomes a little monotonous. So when one meets with interesting people, one is in no hurry to leave. Besides, as I mentioned before, criminology is one of my favorite subjects. We promise to be patient. Tell us of your new insight, I beg. Don't you agree, *mein Schatz*?

"Yes, I would certainly like to know," confirmed Mr. Fontini.

"And you, Ann? Could you endure it?"

"Of course I can," laughed Ann. "I have never seen you like this before. Do you know that you are turning into a virtual male Scheherazade?"

"I prefer to think that is meant as a compliment, and I shall try to be as eloquent as I am able to," countered Bobby McClure with a brief laugh. "Let me see . . . where should we start? It all probably began on the Sunday before High Command threw the bottle against Q2 . . ."

* * *

Chapter 7

Happy Hikers

The first Sunday of June 1975 in Hickory, North Carolina, was one of those days when the Carolina Piedmonts showed itself at its finest. A gentle breeze was blowing, and an abundance of shrubs and trees were still in late bloom. It was the beginning of a long pleasant summer, punctuated by vacations, traveling, yard work, upkeep, sports, and barbecues.

The First Church of the Nazarene on the west side of the town had been newly painted and looked inviting to members and guests, some of whom were now walking out from the annex after completion of the Sunday school classes. They were joined by latecomers arriving from the parking lot and the street. The tightly knit congregation appeared relaxed, greeting and talking with each other as they headed towards the entrance of the sanctuary.

Hank and Lorie Henderson waited on the stairs outside the annex for their son Eric to join them. Hank was a handsome man, thirty-five years old, of average height, and slightly stocky. Dressed in a dark suit, and with his receding hairline offset by a bushy mustache that he had started only recently, one might take him for a banker or a stock broker. His real trade, however, was plumbing. Six years ago, he had started his own plumbing-contractor business which had been doing very satisfactorily, and by now, he had four employees helping him. As he was a deacon of the church, he was well known among its members, and he and Lorie exchanged greetings and handshakes with other parishioners while waiting.

Lorie looked a few years younger than her husband and was dressed in a spring-colored cotton dress and was wearing a hat.

Addressing his wife, Mr. Henderson said, "Do you remember the last time we went to the mountains? I cannot believe how fast time flies. It must have been three years ago . . . maybe four? It was a beautiful day, just like today. Quiet, serene, so full of joy and peace. What was the name of that overlook we hiked up to?"

"Yes, I do remember," answered Mrs. Henderson. "Eric was only eleven then. He is still talking about that spring you showed him in the woods close to the lookout point. I think that it was called Watauga Overlook. Eric was mesmerized by the water seeping out of the rock, so clean that one could drink it right there. He believes that he has never tasted better water. Yes, it was a beautiful place. We ought to go up there again some time soon."

"Hey, son," called Mr. Henderson to Eric, who at last emerged from the annex in busy discussion with another boy they knew well. "Did you learn anything new today?"

"Oh, I don't know," answered Eric. He was well developed for his fourteen years of age. His movements were quick and agile, and his body was built like that of a good athlete. His oval head was highlighted by bright blue eyes, freckles, and a mop of brown hair. "Actually, the teacher talked mostly about baseball and stuff. You know that Mr. Wannamaker, our new Sunday school teacher, is our coach in the Little League baseball team. He is real cool and knows things."

Lorie could not help laughing and exclaimed, "Shame on him. He is old enough to know that the church is not a baseball club. There is more to life than baseball!"

Eric's friend, Howie Worthington, laughed with her and offered apologetically, "He knows that there is, ma'am. But he is very good at putting it all together. He believes that there is a sound mind in a sound body. He also talks about swimming and basketball and running and hiking."

Howie was of about the same height and built as Eric. He had thick curly black hair, a winning smile displaying a set of beautiful white teeth, and regular features. His father was a foreman in one of the furniture factories in the town, and they lived in the same neighborhood as the Hendersons. Howie and Eric attended the same junior high school and played on the same Little League Baseball team which was coached by Mr. Wannamaker. Howie was probably the best pitcher in the league and an important reason why their baseball team was one of the three best in the league.

"Yeah, I will stand up for Mr. Wannamaker any time. He understands us kids," echoed Eric.

"He certainly seems to have your respect, and I admire him for that. But I hope that he also teaches a little about our Lord's redeeming love, at least when he is in the Sunday school class! Well, it is getting late, we better move over to the sanctuary. Would you like to join us, Howie?"

"Sure."

On the short walk, Mrs. Henderson casually spoke to Eric, "Your father was just saying that it would be nice to do another hike up to the Watauga Overlook, you know the place in the mountains we visited three years ago? Would you like to go?"

"Is that not the place where we had lunch on the bare rock? We could see for miles and there was a spring coming out of the side of the mountain?" asked Eric.

"Yes, that's the very place."

"That would be great! Can Howie go too?"

"Of course, if his parents will give their permission. Well, here we are."

It was almost time for the service to begin, and the sanctuary was nearly full. The group spotted a row with only four people and headed for it. It turned out that two of them were Mr. and Mrs. Wannamaker, and the boys sat down next to them, greeting them both. Mr. and Mrs. Wannamaker waved to the Hendersons.

They knew each other quite well from several neighborhood activities.

The organ began with a prelude, and a hush fell over the congregation. The minister, the Reverend James Boling III, was a kind-looking man in his sixties. He was nearly bald now, which made his ruddy-complexioned head seem unusually large and domineering above the black robe. He still had a powerful voice with a warm quality, and usually he was a skillful and inspiring orator. He had been minister for their church for almost eighteen years now, and his approaching retirement was anticipated with regret by the overwhelming majority of the members of the congregation.

As the service came to the sermon, Pastor Boling went behind the pulpit. Spreading his arms, he began, "Friends, listen to our Lord's instructions, as written by his disciple John in the fifteenth chapter and of which there can be no doubt."

He read from the bible: "I am the true vine, and my Father is the gardener. He cuts off every branch in me that bear no fruit, while every branch that does bear fruit He trims clean, so that it will be more fruitful. You are already clean because of the words I have spoken to you. Remain in me, and I will remain in you . . . If anyone does not remain in me and my words remain in you, he is like a branch that is thrown away and withers, such branches are picked up, thrown into the fire and burned. But if you remain in me, and my words remain in you, ask whatever you wish, and it will be given to you . . . My command is this: Love one another as I have loved you. Greater love has no one than this, that one lay down his life for his friends . . . You did not choose, but I chose you to go and bear fruit that will last . . . This is my command: Love each other."

The Reverend James Bowling III continued with his analysis and examples of what was meant by the scripture, using easily understandable language and everyday situations.

After the service, the worshippers filed out slowly. Eric and Howie started a discussion with Mr. Wannamaker as to whether playing baseball qualified as bearing 'fruit.' Mr. Wannamaker was of the opinion that it had to be so, even if baseball had not been known when John wrote his testament. He was supported by his wife, with the qualification that each player had to do his best and play by the rules.

Howie squinted at the Wannamakers and offered that he was not so sure that Mrs. Henderson would agree with their point of view.

Lorie Henderson heard Howie's remark and felt compelled to clarify herself. "No, I have nothing against baseball. I am sure that it teaches the players many good values. But I happen to believe that 'bearing fruit' in this context relates to religious and moral qualities, rather than to sports. No offense, Jack and Jill, for the most part, sports are good for both the soul and the body. And we keep hearing that Jack is doing an outstanding job in that regard."

Jack Wannamaker replied, "Thank you for saying that, Lorie. It's good to see you again. You look fit! How do you manage to stay in such a good condition?"

"For one thing, I go to aerobics, and I play tennis with some of the girls. And occasionally, the whole family goes mountain hiking," replied Lorie Henderson modestly.

"Ah, yes, hiking. There is an enriching sport if you have the legs and the back for it. We used to do that quite often some years back," interjected Jill Wannamaker.

The group was now outside the sanctuary in the clear sunshine. Hank Henderson looked around. "Did you really? I didn't know that! Would you, by any chance, be interested in a day's hiking in the mountains next Tuesday? The forecast predicts that the weather will hold at least through Tuesday, and I could arrange to take the day off. We would be happy to have both of you join us, wouldn't we, Lorie?"

"That would be a treat. We were talking about going to the Watauga Overlook. Eric and Howie plan to join us as well."

"I believe that Tuesday is open, now that school is out," replied Jack Wannamaker. "Do you think that we still can handle it, Jill?"

"Why not, it sounds great."

"Well, it's all planned then. Just bring yourself and Jack's accordion. We will take care of the lunch. Can we pick you up with the station wagon at about seven a.m.?" asked Hank.

"We shall be ready at seven Tuesday morning. And I promise that I will leave my baseball at home," replied Jack with a boyish grin.

* * *

Jack Wannamaker woke up at dawn Tuesday morning. He got out of bed and raised the window shade. He noted with satisfaction that the early morning sky was clear and that only a slight breeze was swaying the tree branches. It looked as if the weather forecaster had been right when he had predicted in last evening's TV newscast that Tuesday would be another sun-filled glorious day.

Jack went into the living room and did a series of calisthenics while still in his pajamas. Although he was in excellent physical condition, he had not done any serious hiking for years, and he wanted to make sure that his leg and back muscles had been stretched and limbered up. During his courtship with Jill and for several years after they had married, they had often gone on hiking trips, sometimes lasting several days. He looked forward to testing himself on this, for him, new trail.

Jack had just turned thirty years old a month ago. He was of about average height and had the harmonious body of a trained gymnast, a sport he had pursued with excellence in his high school and college days. His gray-blue eyes had the youthful sparkle one often finds in persons who have retained a sense of wondering and an eagerness to pursue the great experience of life. His dark blond hair was cut short in the style typical for gymnasts. He had a healthy sense of humor, a good voice, a ready smile, and a high level of confidence.

Before he went to the shower, he returned to the bedroom, shut the alarm clock off, and awoke Jill with a kiss. "Honey! It is time to rise and shine. We have great things to do. Remember?" he said as she opened her eyes.

He had met Jill while they both studied at the same college.

She had enrolled a year after he did, also studying education. Her major had been in biology, which she was now teaching. They had become engaged shortly before Jack graduated, and married just after Jill had finished her education. Fortunately, they had been able to find employment in the same school district in Hickory, North Carolina, Jack in the high school, Jill in one of the junior high schools.

Jill was a pretty brunette with hazel eyes, looking quite studious because of the eyeglasses she usually wore to correct her nearsightedness. She had graduated on top of her class and had a reputation for being an effective teacher, in spite of a natural inclination to be shy. Jack and Jill had decided to wait with starting a family until later, so that she could take advantage of her education.

Jack had coffee and ham omelet ready in the kitchen when Jill showed up, dressed in light blue shorts and a blue-and-green-patterned shirt. "Don't forget 'old Monroe,'" she reminded him, placing a compact accordion on the kitchen table. "Hank explicitly asked that you bring it!"

Old Monroe, so nicknamed after the name of the manufacturer, had been given to Jack as a birthday gift when he was a teenager.

"Good old Monroe? I haven't played you for at least a year!" Jack wiped off some dust from the accordion. "I wonder if I still have the right touch." He put the leather straps around his shoulders and let his fingers run over the keys testing a few notes. Imperceptibly, he keyed into the tune of 'A Happy Wanderer.' "You got it all right," encouraged Jill. "Now play with gusto!"

He stretched the accordion to its maximum and started from the beginning, pressing hard on the end boards and using plenty of bass as well. The melody rang through the whole house as he began to sing, "A happy wanderer am I . . ."

Jill joined in, "Falderi, faldera, falderi, faldera, rah, rah . . ." They both laughed as they finished the verse, and Jack played out the tune.

"If we go on like this, the police may be knocking on the door before long," gagged Jill.

Jack switched tune and began singing,

> "Hail, hail, the gang is here,
> Old girl the gang is here!
> Hail, hail, the gang is here,
> What the heck do we care?"

The doorbell rang. "Now you have done it, Jack," exclaimed Jill, putting a finger to her lips. "I hope that it is not the police!" She went to the front door and opened it.

Hank Henderson was standing outside with a deadpan expression on his face. "Is this 1112 Morningside Drive? We have received several complaints from your neighbors, including the Hendersons at 1204. They seem to fear that you illegally may be keeping wild lions in your home," he inquired.

Jill picked up the mood and answered with feigned guilt, "Oh, no, Officer. We wouldn't do a thing like that. It's just my husband gargling his throat." They both burst into a laughter. "Won't you come in?"

"Well, I just wanted to let you know that the wagon is here and that we are ready anytime you are. And, by the way, I heard that we may have some rain showers late this afternoon. Better bring some rain gear too, just in case," Hank advised.

A few minutes later, Jack and Jill had completed their preparations and left the house. In his knapsack, Jack carried their raincoats, hats, the accordion, field glasses, a supply of apples, and spare socks.

* * *

It was a few minutes past nine when the Hendersons' station wagon rolled into the unpaved parking area adjoining Route 105 and opposite the turnoff to Route 184. Hank parked next to two other cars in the lot, close to the trail entrance, and turned the ignition off.

The trip from Hickory had been smooth. The passengers had

maintained a lively discussion, mostly exchanging stories about past hiking experiences. Eric had prepared Howie for what he could expect on this particular trail. Although Howie had done some hiking with his parents and two sisters before, he was made to understand that the trail they were about to embark on was considerably more demanding than most others. Howard's expectation rose as the car squirmed up the winding road towards and through Blowing Rock on the crest of the first ridge. It was another hour's driving through the mountains before they reached their destination.

They were all in high spirits. Hank and Eric strapped on the two knapsacks the Hendersons had brought with lunch supplies and miscellaneous belongings, and Jack put on his own. They entered the steep staircase leading up to the woods and the trailhead.

* * *

The hiking trail was marked by stripes painted on the tree trunks about a hundred yards apart. On this lower trail, the stripes were white, and a path about a foot and a half wide had been worn by previous hikers through the overgrown forest bottom, baring the underlying red clay mixed with gravel. The hiking party fell into single file. Hank Henderson took the lead position, followed by Eric and Howie. In the middle Lorie and Jill walked closely together, and Jack Wannamaker formed the rear guard.

The trail was mostly traversing uphill, with enough incline to require special effort for each step taken. Fortunately, the ground was mostly dry, providing good traction for the hikers' cleated shoes. However, in some few places, water seepage had made the ground slippery, making the hikers' passage a delicate act of balancing. The trail was flanked on both sides by dense forest with tall trees, the crowns of which formed a solid green canopy above their heads, and allowing only a soft green twilight to filter through. Tallest were an abundance of majestic oak trees, with hickory, beech, and hemlocks filling in at random. Scattered around, wherever they could find a foothold, were some birches, maples, buckeyes, poplars, walnuts and sycamores. The bottom of the woods was richly covered with rhododendrons, mountain laurels, azaleas, low redbuds, ferns, mosses, and mushrooms. What little open space remained, including the edges along the trail, was covered with violets, flocks, and wildflowers, many of them in full bloom.

Except for their own footsteps and heavy breathing, few sounds were heard by the hikers after they had entered the woods. The noises from the highway traffic below were effectively absorbed by the myriad of leaves.

Hank maintained a moderate pace of not more than seventy steps per minute. Even so, the strain of the continuous uphill hiking soon made everyone perspire and pant heavily. Hank called out when they passed a new or unusual kind of tree, shrub, or plant. Except for these announcements or a rare question or comment from someone in the group, little was spoken.

About three quarters of an hour into the hike, first, Lorie and, then, Jill felt their leg muscles beginning to tighten up, and they gradually fell behind the pace. As a result, the distance between Hank and the boys in the lead and the rest of the group opened up.

In many places, a tree had fallen across the trail, forcing the hikers to mount the trunks in order to pass. Lorie and Jill began to take advantage of the downed trunks as an inviting place to sit down for a few minutes and massage their tiring leg muscles, or to catch their breaths under the pretense of enjoying the scenery. Actually, most of the time, the view was obscured by the plethora of vegetation around them.

An hour into the hike, they came to a small opening in the woods, where a number of large rocks were protruding from the ground. Hank and the boys sat down on several of them, waiting for the rest of the party to catch up. When Lorie, Jill, and Jack finally joined them, Hank opened his knapsack and served refreshments while they rested.

After a ten-minute break, the party got on their feet again. This time, Eric took the lead ahead of Howie, followed by Jack and Jill, and finally Lorie and Hank. The first three were obviously in the best physical shape, and the last three, at intervals, shouted for them to slow down the pace, so that they would not fall too far behind.

The forest air was fresh and clean, saturated with the fragrances of moist soil and the numerous plants and trees. As they gradually got higher up on the mountain, the air temperature dropped a few degrees, although that seemingly was not enough to make them perspire any less. Simultaneously, the air became thinner, making breathing a little more difficult. At length, the group found a rhythm which suited everyone, and the train of the six overheated and heavily panting individuals methodically worked itself, one step at a time, up the stony, winding mountain trail.

Having hiked about a mile and a half, the trail forked. They chose the left branch, which was marked with red stripes on the trees. This section was much steeper than the previous one. In a number of places, the trail was a mere collection of scrambled boulders held together with tree roots, and so steep that the hikers had to support themselves by gripping whatever was within reach to pull themselves forward and up. Their progress was further slowed because many of the boulders were slippery from seeping water and mud.

The trail had so far been engulfed in dense forest in all directions. However, gradually, as they arrived at higher altitude, the trees began to thin out, and occasionally, a patch of blue sky became visible. More and bigger rocks now covered the ground, and crooked trees were clinging to the moss-covered surfaces, their spiny roots entangling everything to get a precarious foothold. Withered or half-dead trees were leaning at odd angles or had tumbled, leaving their roots pointing blindly into space, while still being partly enveloped in clumps of dirt.

A few birds flew up as they passed, but they disappeared quickly among the trees to find other resting places. Occasionally a squirrel, a chipmunk, or a porcupine could be heard or seen as they scampered about in the bottom of the forest.

The 'red' trail came to an end in a fairly level area on top of a knoll at an elevation of about 4400 feet. The eastern side of the area was bordered by a steep, bald rocky face about seventy-five feet high. A cold campfire place with charred wood showed that the area had been used for camping, but no one was occupying it presently. The group again sat down on large boulders to catch their breaths. A nearby marker showed that the trail going down the gentle slope on the southwestern side of the campground led to the peaks of Grandfather Mountain, whereas the 'blue' trail exiting on the northern perimeter led to Watauga Overlook, which was three quarter of a mile away.

Knowing that their goal was getting close and refreshed by the short rest, the group started out on the final leg. Hank was again taking the lead, followed by the boys.

The fauna had changed to spruces, pines, and low deciduous trees scattered among thorny underbrush and heather, mossy rocks, and a profusion of small blue and red flowers. As they traversed the pass between two minor peaks, patches of mist and fog enveloped them as the warmer air from the valley to the southwest was forced up the slope and began condensing its moisture when mixing with the cooler air from higher up.

The trail snaked along the mountainside. The thick underbrush on both sides was nearly choking up the footpath, so that the hikers' shoes and socks continuously brushed against the overhanging spiny shoots. On several stretches, the trail ran across huge heaps of jumbled boulders or mounds of shattered rocks, the latter shifting under the weight of the passing hikers. Where shade prevailed, the air felt refreshingly cool.

They had now reached an elevation where there were relatively few trees, and many of them were stunted and deformed. For the first time during the ascent, the hikers were able to get limited views of the valleys unfolding below them. The incline of the terrain lessened, indicating that they were close to the crest.

* * *

Chapter 8

Tale of the Four Spiders

When High Command, in his rearview mirror, saw that the pursuing patrol car was skidding over the side of the road, he felt a great sense of relief. The battle had been won, thanks to his quick thinking and resolute actions. For a few minutes, he could not help but feel a warm glow inside because he, once more, had successfully led the group to a victory, this time, over the annoying pursuers in the patrol car. The glowing was magnified by the outpouring of admiring signals, hooting, and yelling from his companions.

However, he was enough of a realist to remember that he had seen one of the deputies in the patrol car talking into the microphone before it went off the road. He reluctantly concluded that some kind of roadblock or dragnet was likely to be formed up ahead by the law, and which they were likely to encounter in the next five or ten minutes. That was, of course, if they kept driving on! A new problem had arisen, which once more required that he had to come up with a new workable solution. His brain engaged in a furious search for alternatives.

He rationalized that it was unlikely that the deputies in the wrecked patrol car had been able to read their license plates from their distance. Besides, they all had deliberately let mud and grime accumulate on their license plates during their long trip. A description of their group had to be sketchy at best. If the four could somehow vanish unnoticed from the county and the state, he felt certain that the police would never be able to trace them.

The first move would obviously be to slow down, so that they would not attract undue attention from other motorists, and also to maximize the available reaction time. He throttled back and signaled to Crazy and Firebird to pull in behind him and SS. He pondered whether they should break up the foursome to make them less noticeable, but he decided against it. That would only increase the probability that at least one of them got caught, and that was all the fuzz needed to net them all! Furthermore, he knew that Crazy and Firebird were unpredictable at times. No telling what they would get into if left alone! He therefore decided that they initially should go into hiding together, until the situation had cooled off. The next question was: "Where?"

Again, he studied the terrain on both sides of the highway. They were now driving at a leisurely pace, and he was able to get a good impression of the wood-covered hillsides. On his right, the dense woods rose in waves to the crest of a high ridge a couple of miles away. There were few signs of human habitation. On the left, the hills were steeper, but not nearly as high, and occasionally, a small dairy farm could be found close to the highway. He didn't see any paved side roads, but there were a few narrow dirt roads leading up in the direction of the farms. Hiding their heavy motorcycles in the woods wouldn't be easy, as the highway was mostly either cut into the hilly terrain or, in between, built on top of filled-in sections to minimize the changes in grade and with plenty of steep embankments on both sides. Furthermore, the woods were full of compact underbrush and littered with dead trees and branches.

As the group passed the turnoff to Route 184, High Command wondered if they perhaps should turn off there. From the road signs, he got the impression that it was leading to several resort areas and probably dead-ended somewhere in the mountains. He therefore ruled it out as being a potential trap, because there most likely would be many people that might notice them.

The ridge to the right now seemed to decrease in height before another ridge arose further to the north. High Command wondered if there might be a side road leading over the low point between the two ridges, which could be negotiated by their motorcycles. For some distance, he kept looking for tracks or dirt roads in that direction. However, the woods remained closed and impassable by a solid wall of leaves.

At long last, High Command detected a place, nearly hidden, on the right-hand side where a narrow dirt road must have existed a long time ago. It was now completely overgrown with weeds, and the trees had closed above it. To his trained eye, however, it was unmistakable that the ground was relatively level and hard. There were no houses in sight, and at that moment, there was no other traffic in either direction. He signaled to the other riders to follow him as he turned off the highway and headed into the woods following the trace of the old dirt road.

Soon, however, it turned out to be more difficult to drive the heavily loaded road-going motorcycles on the abandoned road than High Command had anticipated. The 'road' was in many places, deeply rutted from erosion, and trees and shrubs had planted themselves.

For about ten minutes, they kept moving on slowly, alternating between driving and dismounting to push their motorcycles around various obstacles before it became obvious to High Command that it was next to impossible to get through the mountain pass by following that route. He found a fairly level minor opening nearby in the woods, and parked his motorcycle there against a tree. The three others followed him, perspiring and panting.

"Let's all take a break," ordered High Command as he reached into his saddlebag for a bottle of inexpensive wine and a box of crackers.

The four sat down munching on the crackers and drinking freely from the wine bottle, which High Command passed around.

Crazy slapped his thighs and laughed. "He, he . . . you really got them, High C, right on the nose. Did you see them wheel around? Best damned shot I have ever seen!"

"I bet that they don't feel too good right now," added Firebird sarcastically. "If it wasn't for you, High C, they probably would have booked us."

"A toast to the genius of High Command. May his victories be many and the setbacks few and temporary," exuberated SS pompously before he put the bottle to his lips.

High Command smiled benevolently at his three companions, obviously enjoying their praises and compliments. He had known SS since their high school years. They had nicknamed him SS because of his fondness for German World War II souvenirs and his sympathies for some of the ideologies of Nazism. His most precious possession was a side knife of the model that had been issued to the SS soldiers, which he habitually carried in its sheath attached to his belt. He usually wore a black shirt and tight pants, the legs of which were stuffed into his long shafted boots of military style. It had been their common interest in motorcycles that had brought them together, and they had participated in many rallies and tours together.

High Command had known Crazy and Firebird for about three years. They just seemed to have attached themselves to SS and High Command during a rally in Binghamton, New York, and they had been accepted because of their willingness to take part in whatever he and SS had proposed.

After they had finished talking about the disabling of the patrol car, the discussion turned into how they best could escape the deputies, who probably by now were on the lookout for them.

"I had hoped that the track would lead behind the mountain, which it probably does! But it looks like we won't be able to drive that way on the bikes."

"We could walk, if we had to?" proposed Crazy.

"Jezz! You wouldn't want to leave the bikes here, man?" bellowed Firebird.

"Well, we could come back in a few days and pick them up. No big deal!"

"What if the fuzz find them in the meantime?" questioned SS.

"We will just have to hide them and cover the tracks, naturally." Crazy shrugged his shoulders.

"How long would you say the fuzz would keep looking for us, High Command?" asked SS.

"That's the big unknown. I don't know how they work it down here! A day . . . maybe two, if I were to guess. They have other things to do. We are just small fish!" High Command lifted his hands.

"Would it not make sense to stay right here with the bikes and wait for a day or two? Then we could leave the same way we came. Tennessee or Virginia is less than an hour's drive. We have sleeping bags and enough food," proposed Firebird.

High Command, who had just helped himself to a deep swig from the bottle, passed it on to Firebird and asked for a map. SS produced one of the kind offered at state welcome centers. High Command studied it carefully for a while.

"You guys have come up with some pretty good ideas. Let me outline a master plan, and then let's discuss it and hear if you can come up with anything that's better. First, we should conceal the motorbikes right here with branches and leaves and wipe out any tracks we have made. Do a good job at it. Then we will leave together with enough food and drink for the day, heading uphill to some place where we can get a good view of the highway, and see what the fuzz is up to. Needless to say that we should try to avoid being seen by anyone. If it looks like the fuzz doesn't discover our bikes, we will return to this place by sunset, and then drive out one by one with about fifteen minutes intervals." He put a finger on the map. "By morning, we will all meet here in Abingdon, Virginia, at the interchange of I-81 and Route 19. We will take different routes to Abingdon, which we will agree on before we leave. However, in the event that the fuzz do discover the motorbikes before sunset, we may have a bad situation and we'll have to work out some contingency plan. But first, let's see what happens between now and late afternoon!"

"Contingency plan? What the hell do you mean by that?" Crazy asked nervously.

High Command looked calmly at his companions. "Don't

worry, we will think of something. OK, let's get on with hiding the bikes and wiping out the tracks."

* * *

The column of the four motorcycle riders worked itself deeper and deeper into the woods along the abandoned logging road. The road itself was barely detectable, as it was covered thickly with dead leaves and branches, and crisscrossed by toppled rotting trees. In places, the undergrowth was so prolific that they had to force their way through it. The winding logging road continued uphill through the woods, which kept obscuring any view of the highway below. The sky as well remained hidden beyond the massive ceiling of leaves.

An uncomfortable thought had seized High Command, who was walking in the lead. What if the deputies found their motorcycles and had brought dogs to follow their scent? How many dogs might they have? The only weapons in their possession were their side knives and, of course, their hands. They could resort to using sticks or throwing rocks, if necessary. He finally concluded that it was highly unlikely that a small county's sheriff department would have a dog pound of its own. If needed, they would probably have to requisition dogs from a larger town's police department, and that would take valuable time. Furthermore, it was most unlikely that the fuzz would be able to find the hidden motorbikes!

The group sat down resting after they had walked about a mile to the east and reached the crest of the first and lowest ridge. The vegetation here was not quite as dense as it was further down, and they were able to see patches of the surrounding landscape. Towards the west were a few limited views, framed by treetops, of a short stretch of Route 105. They watched the traffic on the highway for about ten minutes, while sipping a little bourbon from the bottles they had brought with them. As far as they could observe, there were no police or patrol cars passing. One particular opening revealed a short section of the highway, which High Command estimated was the place where they had turned off, and he noted with a feeling of triumph that there were no stopped or parked cars to be seen.

To the east, the landscape descended into a shallow depression, in the bottom of which a stream was barely visible, perhaps half a mile away. Judging distances in the mountains is often deceiving! On the other side of the stream, the terrain again rose steeply.

To the north and south stretched the two ridges they had seen from the highway. They both appeared to be significantly higher than their present observation point. The crest of the south ridge increased in heigth farther south, and the vegetation at top level was much less dense than where they were. Near the crest of that ridge High Command noticed a lonely rocky bluff facing northwest, perhaps a little more than a mile away when measured in a straight line. From that point, he estimated, there should be an excellent view of at least five miles of Route 105, including the turnoff point to the hiding place of their motorcycles.

"What do you guys say to spending the day on that bluff up there, just watching the scenery?" asked High Command.

"That is one hell of a climb," grumbled Crazy.

"The exercise will do you good. Besides, High Command is right. It would be the best position for following the movements of the fuzz," opined SS.

"Exercise, my foot! We have had enough exercise for a whole month already!" asserted Crazy.

"It's as simple as this," reasoned High Command. "We have the whole afternoon to kill. But unless we know for sure that the fuzz have lost our trail by evening, it would be stupid to get back on the highway. I bet you a dollar to a doughnut that from that bluff up there, we will have the perfect view of what the fuzz is up. I don't see any other good choices!"

Reluctantly, Crazy screwed the cap back on his bottle and returned it to his pocket. He was cursing to himself as he got up and followed the others.

* * *

"What a magnificent job," exclaimed Jack Wannamaker in awe, as the hiking party arrived at the Watauga Overlook and suddenly faced the vast panorama of majestic mountain chains, the open sky, with floating puffy clouds, and woods covering the landscape as far as the eye could see. With the sun at zenith, the air clean and clear, and a gentle and refreshing breeze, it was easy to believe that one had entered Shangri-La.

They all sat down, partly to admire the scenery, but also to rest their tired limbs and backs and getting cooled off. Notwithstanding that the last half mile to the overlook had been less steep, the thinner air combined with their sustained toil had worn them out.

Howie almost shouted with excitement, "Gosh, I never knew that there were places like this!"

"There are many," Eric answered with an air of worldliness. "But this is one of the better ones."

"Well, I bet that you have worked up a good appetite after all that hiking, Eric and Howie! How about giving me a hand with collecting some firewood for the grill?" suggested Hank Henderson. The boys jumped up, ready to help him.

Together they went into the surrounding woods, and before long, they had collected an assortment of twigs and dead tree branches, which the winter storms had downed. They broke them into smaller pieces and placed them in the fireplace in the center of the overlook. Before long, a deep bed of glowing charcoal went shimmering in the air above it.

While Hank Henderson prepared the hot dogs and the hamburgers on a grill he had mounted above the fire and Lorie Henderson served iced tea and arranged the cardboard plates, cups, and relishes, Jack Wannamaker took his accordion from his backpack and asked if anyone would like to sing along.

From his station at the fireplace, Hank requested, "Why don't you and Jill start with 'Shennendoah'? I still remember how well you did it at the party of the Grunenwalds a couple of years ago."

"Why not? We will start with 'Shennendoah.' Feel free to join us if you like." Jack began to play the introductory notes on his accordion. Jill joined Jack's baritone, as they sang the old sentimental and difficult song:

> Oh Shennendoah, I long to hear you,
> Away you rolling river.
> Oh, Shennendoah, I long to hear you.
> Away I am bound to go,
> 'Cross the wide Missouri . . .

After the verses of "Shennendoah," Jack proposed they should all sing "Three Blind Mice" as a round. He split the group into three duos, the Wannamakers, the Hendersons, and the boys, in a contest to decide which pair had the strongest voices. Having finished, and after much excited discussion, it was mutually agreed that the contest had been a draw, and the party relaxed while eating lunch.

"You know, I could spend all day just sitting here and watching the cloud formations, the lights and shadows, the birds flying by! What else does a person need?" exclaimed Jack Wannamaker with a satisfied sigh.

"Yes, we have been blessed with a beautiful day. On the other hand, I am sure that it can be most unpleasant up here on some occasions," added Lorie.

"Mom, can I show Howie the spring?" asked Eric after the meal was over. "He says that he would like to see it."

"Do you think that you can find the way alone, Eric?"

"Sure! We just go back the way we came a quarter of a mile and turn left on the footpath, until we come to the bare rock where the spring is."

"All right. But be back here in an hour at the latest, Eric. And be careful!" admonished his mother.

The boys got up and were gone.

"Eric seems to have an obsession for that spring," Lorie smilingly explained to Jill.

"Boy, a little nap is all I need now," mumbled Hank, slumping back and resting his head on one of the knapsacks. He closed his eyes.

"Why not? Go ahead, Hank," replied Jack, leaning back against a large boulder. "I will just sit here and make sure that the view doesn't disappear."

Above Jack's head, a black hawk was soaring gracefully back and forth in the updrafts from the mountainside. The bird's head was jerking from side to side, as it was watching the earthbound creatures below. Addressed to Hank, he said, "Look at the hawk up there. How would you like to spend the afternoon flying with it? Such marvelous freedom." But Hank merely grunted in response.

Jack thought that he heard voices yodeling expertly from somewhere in the mountains. He took his binoculars from the knapsack and scanned the terrain, trying to locate the yodelers, but he was unable to find them.

* * *

In his mind's eye, High Command had charted a course from the old logging road to the rocky bluff, where they intended to spend the afternoon. To bypass several gaping crevasses near the crest, he planned to traverse the mountain side to an outcropping knoll further to the south. From there, the terrain leading to the bluff appeared to be reasonably accessible. The total hiking distance, he estimated, should be not more than a mile and a half, assuming that they did not encounter unforeseeable major obstacles.

High Command was himself an experienced mountain hiker. When roaming in the Catskills, the Adirondacks, the Poconos, and on some of the Pennsylvania ridges, he had learned to trust his homing instinct, and his reading of the lay of the terrain had always been excellent. On some of those trips, SS had been with him, and he had come to respect SS's physical strength and his resilience in face of the rigors of mountain hiking. However, he knew less about Firebird's and Crazy's abilities to negotiate mountainous terrain, and he watched them closely to make sure that they did not overexert themselves.

It soon became obvious that Firebird and, in particular, Crazy were straining hard in the overgrown pathless terrain. High

Command tried to conserve their strength by making frequent stops, at which times the two would slump to the ground under much groaning and complaining. By now, all four had taken their jackets off, which did not prevent them from perspiring profusely. In an apparent attempt to ease their bodily aches, both Firebird and Crazy had treated themselves with generous swigs from their bourbon bottles.

Realizing their state of exhaustion, High Command finally asked if they wanted to abandon the ascent. At that time they had reached the lower end of the knoll southwest of the bluff. From that position, there was no view of Route 105 and the environs where they had parked their motorcycles. Without hesitation, SS advised that they should continue, even if Firebird and Crazy had to be helped on the remaining short distance to the bluff, and he felt certain that they would be sufficiently recovered to hike down on their own power by evening. After another lengthy break, Firebird and Crazy finally agreed to go on.

As their procession approached the bluff and the grade of the terrain lessened, Firebird's and Crazy's frame of mind improved somewhat. Or perhaps the reason had something to do with the liquor they had consumed? The group finally arrived at narrow footpath, which High Command surmised would lead to the appointed observation point.

After leaving Route 105, they had not seen nor heard any other people, and none were in sight on the footpath either. They took another rest and discussed what their reaction should be in case they encountered people. High Command's view, at length, prevailed, which was that he and SS would hand their jackets to Firebird and Crazy, who then were to make themselves invisible in the underbrush, while the two others proceeded boldly in full sight. When the path was clear again, High Command and SS would return and rejoin with the other two.

However, as they followed the footpath, they did not meet with anyone. It appeared as if they had the whole mountain undisturbed for themselves.

High Command looked at the sky and, from the position of

the sun, estimated the time to be about one o'clock. Further west, he spotted a black hawk lazily soaring in the thermals above the bluff. On seeing the bird, he mumbled to himself, "How much easier it would have been if you could do the scouting and tell us?"

* * *

Eric and Howie walked back on the trail they had previously come by. It was winding and hemmed in on both sides by trees and underbrush, but the downhill slope made their walking fast. Even as they were forced to walk in single file, Eric in the lead, they could easily talk together without raising their voices. Apart from the rustling of leaves, all was quiet.

"Have you seen a real spring before?" asked Eric.

"Not that I remember. Except perhaps for some muddy places where water seeps out of the dirt," answered Howie.

"Did you know that many mountains are full of water inside, and that you can see it trickle out through the surface, enough to form small brooks? The water that comes out is clean and cold. If you want to, you can drink it. It's cleaner than the water you get in your home."

"How can the mountain be full of water? Rocks are hard and solid, not like a sponge!"

"Very true. But there are millions of tiny cracks and holes in the mountains, where rainwater gets trapped. I have been told that sometimes there are whole rivers of water inside a mountain! Well, here is where we turn off. We will be there in a few minutes!"

They turned left on a barely visible trail, which kept winding downhill among scattered large boulders. The tree branches again closed above their heads, making everything look dark green and mysterious.

"Are there any snakes here?" asked Howie with sudden alarm in his voice.

"Nope! It's too cold up here in the winter. Further down, you may find some. But we may meet with some mice and squirrels, if we are lucky. Hey, look at this! A giant spider's web!"

Between two trees, a spider had spun a web across the trail, nearly three feet in diameter. The boys stopped and studied it.

"Are spiders poisonous?" asked Howie with some trepidation.

"Some are, I know. See, the spider is sitting in the corner, waiting for a catch." Eric took a twig from the ground and touched the web gently in the middle. The spider, sensing the impact, immediately rushed towards the area that Eric had touched. "If it had been an insect hitting the web, the spider would have spun a cocoon around it and paralyzed it with poison to keep it fresh. That way, the spider would have enough food stored up for some time. Sorry, old spider, this time, there won't be any dinner for you," laughed Eric.

"Yeah, it looks mean and ugly. Let's get away from that web."

They inched their way around the web, careful not to touch it, and proceeded down the trail.

"I wonder if a spider's poison can kill people."

"Yes, some spiders' can, or at least make people very sick. Just like the poisons from scorpions or snakes can. Some spiders grow very big, especially in the jungles. I have seen that on movies," replied Eric knowingly.

"Yeach," exclaimed Howie with a bodily shiver. Then on a sudden impulse he asked, "Would it be a sin to kill spiders? Pastor Boling says that killing is a sin."

"Gosh, I don't think so. Not anymore than swatting a fly or a mosquito or an ant. I would think that even Pastor Boling does that once in a while. I think that he means that killing people is a sin. Why don't you ask Mr. Wannamaker when we get back? He ought to know!"

"Then, do you think that God created the spiders?"

"Yeah! He created everything."

"I wonder why. What good do they do?"

"I don't know. No one ever told me. I suppose they must be good for something."

"Like what?"

"Can't think of anything. They are just here!"

"You know? I think that he should not have done that. They are just mean and ugly. Yeach!"

The trail ended at a small brook with a swift flow of clear cool water. Eric turned to the left and pointed to a large bare area on the nearly vertical mountain wall fifty yards away. "That's where the water is coming from. Follow me, Howie," he said as he ducked and picked his way through the underbrush.

As they were standing in front of the wall, they could see water seeping out from many fissures in the surface. Below the drippings united into many small streams, which disappeared under the stones and gravel on the ground and later reemerged as the beginning of the brook. Eric went over to one of the streams and filled his cupped hands with water, which he drank from several times. "Try it yourself. It is good water!"

"Boy, that is super!" agreed Howie after he had tasted the cool mountain water. "Thank you for showing me this spring, Eric."

Having satisfied their thirst, they sat down on a fallen tree trunk and looked at the wall for a while. Howie pointed to a place on it and challenged Eric, "Do you see that brown spot up there, Eric? I will give you ten to eight throws from behind this tree trunk that I can hit it more often than you can."

Eric studied the oval target, which was about two feet wide by a foot and a half tall, located on the wall about nine feet above their heads. Somehow, the rock face had changed its color from its predominant dark gray to a bright ochre brown that stood out very clearly. It was about forty feet away from the fallen tree trunk. Eric weighed the odds carefully, knowing that Howie was a considerably better pitcher than himself. Finally, he answered, "Give me ten to seven, and I am game."

"OK, that is fair enough," agreed Howie. "You go first. We both have two free throws to get a feel for the distance."

Eric picked up a small supply of stones from the ground, each about two or three inches in size, and positioned himself behind the fallen tree trunk. Having thrown the first rock, he realized that it would be difficult to hit the target, which was at an unusual angle. His second throw was better, hitting within two feet of the brown target.

"All right, we'll start to count now," warned Howie, as Eric was ready to throw the third time.

Eric got very excited when his stone hit the target. "One out of one!" he shouted.

Of the remaining nine throws, he was not as skilled or lucky. Only one more stone hit within the target area, and another hit on the fringe and caused considerable discussion before they agreed to count it as half a point.

"Not bad," said Howie. "Two and a half will be tough to beat. Let me warm up with two free throws too."

Howie hit the target on the fringes with both stones. "Must be the light!" he mumbled to himself and selected several more stones with care. "Well, here goes."

Howie's next stone was low by several feet. He clenched his teeth and changed his stance to get better footing. The following stone impacted next to the spot of Eric's disputed hit, and they agreed to count it as half a point. Of the remaining five rocks, three were unquestionably within the target area.

"I should have known! Three and a half wins over my two and a half. Good show, Howie. No wonder that you are chosen most often as the pitcher." Eric shook Howie's hand sportily. "How do you do it?"

"Practice, practice, practice!" answered Howie with sly grin. "After a while, you can feel it in your muscles and in your head. It also helps to pitch hard, so the stone won't have time to drop too far. You could easily get the same feel for it if you pitch as often as I do. Come, let's have another game. I'll give you ten to six."

* * *

With High Command in the lead, they came to a fork in the trail. The right branch ran south, following the general direction of the crest of the mountain. A marker on the left branch read: "Watauga Overlook 1/4 mile." He motioned to the others to stay behind as he went up the left branch to reconnoiter.

As he approached the end of the trail, he could hear women's voices. Trying to stay out of sight, he went through the underbrush to a place with large boulders higher up, from where he could get a view of the activities on the overlook. He counted four persons occupying the gently sloping rocky ledge about ten feet below him. Two were women wearing shorts in the process of collecting the remains from a recent meal and packing them into a knapsack. A man was lying down in apparent sleep, and another man was sitting on a boulder near the far end with his back to High Command, watching the scenery through binoculars. From where the last one was sitting, one would have an unobstructed panoramic view of a long section of the highway, as well as the woods where their motorcycles were hidden. High Command silently cursed the presence of the four people and looked around in the hope of finding alternate nearby sites with a similar good view. He concluded that there were no options out of sight of the four occupants. He silently cursed again and returned to his companions without being discovered.

"We've got a little complication," he said after he had rejoined them in the underbrush at the trail fork. "The overlook is already occupied by two couples. There is no telling how long they will stay, but it could be quite a while. One of the guys is sleeping right now. The view from the bluff is ideal, but we can't get there without being discovered. And, unfortunately, it looks like there is no other suitable observation point nearby out of sight of the four. What do you think?"

There was a long pause while everybody pondered the possibilities. Crazy was the first to offer an opinion. "I would say, let's wait here until they clear out. As long as we don't have to walk back on that damned mountain. I have had it up to here with walking! What is the rush? There is plenty of time until sunset. They will probably leave before long."

Firebird chimed in next. "What's wrong with a little dough? How much do you figure they are good for, High C?"

"I don't have the slightest! Perhaps fifty or one hundred bucks at the most! They don't look like millionaires! "But don't forget that we are playing possums. They undoubtedly would blabber to the fuzz if they learn too much about us. Especially if they get off the mountain before we do."

"Yeah! Damn!" replied Firebird.

Another pause followed. SS unsheathed his knife and turned it between his fingers as if he was studying it carefully. Finally, he suggested casually, "We could knock them off. That would be the simple solution."

Crazy jumped up in excitement. "Now it's you who are crazy like a jackass, SS," he hissed. "Knocking four people off for fifty bucks? You are out of your mind! The fuzz would be looking for us all over the country."

"Quiet down, man. Simmer down or you will give us away! Those dudes are only a couple of hundred yards away, you know," admonished High Command.

"Well, couldn't they accidentally fall from the bluff? No, that wouldn't look natural if all four did it," SS corrected himself. Turning to Crazy, he continued, "I didn't know that you were suffering from moral scruples. We could hide the bodies in the woods. It may be years before they were found, if ever."

Crazy shook his head and tried to steady himself with another swig from the bottle. His hands were shaking badly.

"Hey, fellows, we aren't getting anywhere," interrupted High Command impatiently. "OK, here is our situation again. We have decided to spend the afternoon here on the mountain, keeping close watch on the fuzz, right? Now, if it looks like the fuzz have lost us or given up trying to find us, we will return to the bikes in the late afternoon and leave one by one after dark. Right? Now, the problem is that we cannot get a good look at the highway without being seen by those dudes who are camping on the only available good observation point in sight, and it is getting too late in the day to try and find another one. Right? And, besides, even if we decide to look for another suitable lookout point, there may not be any. Right? Or, even if there is, what are our chances of stumbling onto it? It seems simple enough to me! We have two choices. Either the group stays in hiding here and we take turns sneaking up behind the lookout for brief snatches of views of the highway, as best as we are able to, hopefully without being discovered, or we can move in and immobilize the campers in some way, so that they can't give us away, at least not until we are safely out of the state. The weaknesses of the first plan is, one, that we cannot observe very effectively if we have to stay in hiding from those people on the overlook. And, two, that they may accidentally discover us anyway. The weakness of the second plan is that we don't know if other people may arrive later on, in which case we would have to immobilize them too. Right? Is that so complicated? Pick your choice!"

"And what do we mean with 'immobilize'?" asked Firebird, staring into the ground.

"Oh, something that will keep the campers up here for at least twenty-four hours, or maybe more. Like tying them up to some trees, for example." High Command pulled out a length of rope from one of his pockets. "This would do. We might gag them too so they cannot shout, although I doubt that anyone would show up here today after we leave. No, I agree with Crazy that knocking them off would be a last resort only, say, if they, for example, became obstinate, or if some other complication came up. I also value my freedom. My hunch is that they would be scared stiff and cooperate fully!"

"If you ask me, I will vote for the first plan. Let's stay in hiding," offered Crazy.

"No guts," responded SS with sarcasm showing. "I vote for the second plan. Let's go and get'm."

"And what is your choice, Firebird?" asked High Command as Firebird remained silent.

"Damned if I know!" Firebird finally mumbled while shrugging his shoulders. "You got us into this bloody mess. Now find a way to get us out! Whatever you decide is good enough for me, I guess."

"Hey, man. Wait a minute. We are all in this together. Let's have no hard feelings. The first law of survival is sticking together. If we cannot do that, we might as well just walk back to the highway and turn ourselves over to the fuzz." High Command's tone of voice sounded as if he felt personally wounded.

He then continued in his usual confident manner, "I'll wager that those dudes are harmless and probably the only people on the mountain, other than ourselves. We have clear superiority and the element of surprise. Remember that our getting away from here without being detected and caught depends on us knowing what is going on down there on that highway. Do you read me, Firebird?"

"If you say so, High C," mumbled Firebird.

"And you, Crazy? Are you with us?"

Crazy looked glassy eyed on High Command and finally croaked, "I am, as long as there is no killing."

"I don't think that will be necessary," replied High Command. "Just let me do the talking. They will understand what is best for them. All you have to do is to back me up with your knives in hand and to make sure that no one attempts to run away. Should visitors show up later, we will give them the same treatment. Isn't that simple enough?"

"Clear as crystal," agreed SS. The other two remained silent.

* * *

Chapter 9

The Confrontation

Lorie and Jill had finished packing the leftover food and the utensils into one of the knapsacks. The waste paper had been thrown into the fireplace and was burning brightly on the still-glowing embers. Jill extracted two apples from Jack's knapsack and handed one to Lorie. Talking together, they leaned comfortably back against a slanted offset in the overlook, while facing the spectacular view of the mountains.

The piece and quiet was suddenly broken by the sounds of heavy boots landing on the hard surface of the overlook. Lorie and Jill turned their heads by the unexpected noise and noticed four men dressed in jeans and black jackets, each holding a knife pointed at them, and quickly spreading out. "Good God, who are they?" gasped Lorie.

One of the men with short blond hair and hard blue eyes walked quickly towards Lorie. Placing his knife against the skin of her neck, he commanded her to stand up. Shaken, she arose and looked confused at him. He twisted her left arm behind her back and moved his knife against her spine.

The commotion alerted Jack, and he jumped down from the

boulder. Discovering that Lorie was held hostage by one of the intruders, he shouted angrily, "Let go of her, you scum!"

Another of the men, tall and powerfully built, and with shoulder-length brown hair, lifted his knife threateningly towards Jack. "Stay where you are and watch your language, unless you want to see her hurt."

Hank had awoken from his sleep and sat up while trying to grasp what all the shouting was about. Eyeing his wife, he shouted anxiously, "Lorie, are you all right?" and stumbled onto his feet.

"Quiet! You all be quiet!" commanded the tall intruder with authority. "Listen carefully. If you all cooperate, no one is going to get hurt, including the lady here." He pointed to Lorie. "If on the other hand you cause any problems for us . . ." He did not finish the sentence, but made instead a telling gesture by moving his knife in front of his own throat. "And I mean any problems. Let there be no doubt about it. Do exactly what we tell you. If you resist or try to escape or yell or signal for help . . ." He repeated the gesture with the knife in front of his throat. "You all understand that or do I need to repeat it? You are doing good! Now I have a few favors to ask of you. First, throw your wallets over here to me and remember what I just told you."

Seething inside, Jack reached for his wallet and threw it contemptuously towards the tall stranger. It landed at High Command's feet, who picked it up, looked into it, and stuck it into a rear pocket on his jeans.

"I th . . . I think mine is in the knapsack," stammered Hank. "Shall I go and get it?"

"You stay where you are," answered High Command and pointed to Jill. "You there, go and get it for me."

Jill went over to the knapsack on which Hank had been resting his head while sleeping. She found the wallet in one of the outside compartments and threw it to the tall intruder.

"Good," said High Command picking up the wallet. "Is that all the money you have with you?"

Both Hank and Jack nodded.

"OK, we will check into that later." High Command pointed

at Jack and ordered, "You walk slowly to the tree over there. I will follow you, so don't try any funny stuff." Addressed to Firebird, he asked, "Will you show him the way?"

Firebird walked over to the southwestern fringe of the overlook where there were a few low trees and a thin groundcover. He selected a wind-twisted tree with several strong branches close to the ground and motioned for Jack to sit down with his back against the trunk. While High Command looked on, Firebird tied Jack's wrists to two branches with pieces of rope. When finished, High Command inspected the ropes to ensure that the knots were tight. He then shouted to Hank, "OK, you come over here now."

Hank, visibly shaken, staggered across the rough ground to the two men, who in the meantime had selected another tree bordering on the overlook and separated by about twenty feet from Jack's. "Sit down there," ordered High Command.

Firebird pulled two more pieces of rope from a pocket and tied Hank's wrists to strong branches about two feet above the ground. Again, High Command inspected the ropes and instructed the two male prisoners, "You probably won't mind to sit here for a while. Don't forget what I told you. If there are any troubles, you are goners and so is your lady friend over there. We will be keeping an eye on you, so just behave like good boys!"

High Command then returned to Jack and touched his bare chest just above the shirt opening with the tip of his knife. Looking into Jack's eyes, he snarled, "I have your number, buddy. What you called my friend was not very nice." He put pressure on the knife, so it barely penetrated Jack's skin. "He is kind of proud and is easily offended. If you make any more snide remarks like that, I don't think that I can stop him from slicing you up like a salami!"

Satisfied with the effect of his bravado High Command quickly flicked his knife upward, passing its point within a fraction of an inch of Jack's nose and eyes, and then put it back in its sheath. He removed the binoculars still hanging by the strap around Jack's neck, and he and Firebird returned to where SS was still holding Lorie with her arm behind the back.

Addressing SS, he said, "Things are under control now, but

keep guarding her and make sure she doesn't do anything foolish. Tie her up if necessary." Then turning to Firebird, he continued, "And you keep watch on that other dame. Don't let them talk to each other, keep them apart! I've got a little bird watching to do."

High Command went over to the large boulder only a few feet inside the periphery of the overlook, which Jack had previously occupied. He climbed up and made himself comfortable before lifting the binoculars to his eyes and adjusting them so that the highway in the valley came into sharp focus.

* * *

Lorie felt that her guardian let go of her arm. Although still frightened, she turned to face him. He was putting the knife back in the sheath at his right hip, followed by taking off his vinyl jacket. She estimated that he was about five feet eleven inches tall. The face was regular, and he appeared to be in his late twenties. "Let's sit down over there," he told her casually, pointing to a fairly level area about twenty feet north of the entrance. After they had seated themselves, the man took a pint-size bottle from a pocket in his jacket and took a slow sip from it. He then suggestively held the bottle out towards Lorie, as if asking her to help herself to a drink.

"No, thank you. I've just had tea," she said.

"Suit yourself." He replaced the cap on the bottle and put it back to where it came from.

"Would you mind telling me who you are?"

"That wouldn't be very clever, wouldn't it? But you may call me Jim, if you want to."

"Very well, Jim. I am Lorie Henderson and married to Hank over there. How long are you going to stay here?"

"Depends . . . Hard to say. Maybe four or five hours."

"Is it necessary for you to keep us prisoners for all that time? The overlook is open to the public. Anyone can visit or leave as they want!"

"Let's say that we like your company for as long as we are here."

"Is someone after you?"

His face tensed, and he snapped, "No, of course not! But don't ask any more questions. I will do all the questioning that's needed. Just lie down and be quiet!"

Lorie reclined on the rough hard surface. She remembered that Eric and Howie had left half an hour earlier and should return before too long. She wondered how the boys would react when they discovered what the situation was on the overlook, and how they, in turn, would be treated. Her earlier anxieties and fears surfaced again. As was her habit, when she was under stress, she folded her hands and prayed silently to God that He would arrange everything according to His will. Even so, she began to feel an intense dislike for these four savage individuals. Surely, she reasoned, they could not be Christians, nor any kind of God-fearing people. She asked herself whether the strangers' souls might be saved. Having been promised eternal heavenly life after earthly death, she was not particularly afraid of dying. But what would happen if they were maimed or crippled by these hoodlums? She also felt a heavy responsibility for Howie. What would she say to his parents, who had entrusted their only son to her? She felt her heart pounding hard again, and a feeling of nausea came over her.

She opened her eyes slightly to look at her guard. He was still sitting there next to her, and with his eyes resting on her. He had that bottle in his hand again! She quickly closed her eyes and tried to pray again. But so many other thoughts kept rushing through her mind that she had difficulty concentrating on the praying. Were the strangers in some kind of compact with the devil? There had to be some way of getting rid of them. *Strike them down with your bolt of lightning . . . Show us your miraculous power . . . Deliver us from evil. For thine is the kingdom, and the power, and the glory . . . forever . . . and ever . . .*

* * *

"OK, chick," ordered the stranger, taking hold of Jill's arm. "You heard what the man said. Come with me." He led her to the middle of the overlook and had her sit down leaning against a raised rock slab four or five yards from the fireplace and about midway between Lorie and Hank. He sheathed his knife, removed his jacket, belched loudly, and sat down a few feet away from her, resting his back against the same slab.

Jill noticed immediately that the man was far from being sober. His eyelids and jaw was drooping, and he had difficulty speaking coherently. She estimated him to be about five feet ten inches tall, and probably weighing about 165 pounds. He had long tousled bronze-colored hair, a face full of stubble and marked with several scars, prominent teeth, and a poor posture. She estimated his age to be about twenty-five years.

She leaned against the rock slab, removed her glasses, and closed her eyes. The picture of Jack with a knife against his chest kept flashing through her mind. Was he hurt? Who were these thugs? Why did they want to stay on the overlook? They had stolen their money, was that not enough? What more could they want? How were they going to treat their captives, and how would this end?

She felt tears of anger and frustration coming to her eyes. *No*, she decided, *I must not cry!* She would not give the thugs that satisfaction too. She had to force herself not to cry. It was ironic that Jack, with his beautiful liberal mind and being liked so mush by just about everybody, had been taken a lowly prisoner. He had every right to call that thug a 'scum.' Yes, they were all scums!—*No, stay in, you tears!*

She asked herself what she could do to improve their situation. Were there any options other than just waiting and hoping for the best? Her thinking went back to her college classes in psychology. Was it possible to make these men change their intentions? It seemed obvious that the tallest of them was their leader. The others behaved subserviently and probably feared him, at least in secrecy. He did seem resolute and organized, but how rationally might he function in everyday situations? His weakness, she thought, was probably an inflated ego. An egomaniac with a desperate emotional need to dominate and feel respected by others. Could she flatter him into his senses? She decided that it was a long shot, but worth a try.

She put her glasses back on and turned to her guard. "Sir, could I have a word with your leader?" she asked.

"Huh?" was the answer from the slumping guard.

"I wondered if you would mind to ask your leader if I could talk with him, please?"

"About what?"

"About us and the whole situation."

"Fat chance. Why should he?"

"Perhaps we can come to some kind of a bargain," insisted Jill.

"A deal? Well, if you want to, I can ask him. But don't try to run away!" He motioned to the fourth intruder to look out for Jill and walked unsteadily over to the leader, who was still studying the valley intensely through the binoculars.

The audience was short, and Jill's guard returned within a minute. "He is not interested. He thinks that you are trying to trick us," reported the guard tersely, dropping into his previous sitting position.

A paranoid, sadistic, despotic egomaniac, concluded Jill. *Is there any way of getting through to such a person other than with bullets? . . . Now, what else?*

She closed her eyes again and tried to analyze the situation from many angles. There seemed to be only two small openings, she concluded. First, she might appeal to the guard and win his sympathy. But even if she was successful in doing so, what influence might he have with the others? Second, would the boys run for help after they returned and discovered what had happened? That is, of course, if they were not first discovered themselves and caught by the hoodlums. Help from whom? The nearest telephone was back at the highway, hours away! The only possible outcome seemed to be that nothing would change, until the men themselves decided to leave. *There is nothing I can personally do except waiting.* Even so, she again turned to her guard and said politely, "Thank you for asking anyway. I really didn't expect he would be willing to listen to me. He seems like a sort of an odd fellow. Do you find your leader easy to get along with?"

He looked at her with a surprised glance and answered

brusquely, "None of your business, lady! Just shut up and stop thinking."

* * *

Jack felt his head spinning. The ropes held his hands tied firmly to the branches, and the uneven tree trunk was biting into his back. Never before in his life had he been confronted with such naked abusive power. He had only known competition based on a desire to win, and it had always been in accordance with the rules of fair play. Simply submitting to brute force without being able to counter the challenge was a new experience for him.

In his mind, he criticized himself for not having put up a fight. Although he had never participated in any of the sports which might have been useful in self defense, his body was still strong and in excellent physical shape. Had he resisted, chances were that he would have been hurt or worse and that the hoodlums might have hurt Lorie or Jill in retaliation. However, he still wondered if he at least should have tried against the odds. It infuriated him that he had allowed himself to be intimidated by those vicious strangers.

He still felt the stinging pain of the knife prick in his chest. He looked down and noticed a small blood smear on his shirt. It doesn't look like anything dangerous, he concluded, but he still remembered the icy warning by the hoodlums' leader, "I have your number." Inside his mind, Jack fumed, *I have your number too, you scum. You will pay for this. Somehow . . .*

Then Jack checked himself in his thinking. *Good God, am I not teaching the youngsters to turn the other cheek when abused? Don't I have an obligation to practice what I am teaching? Does it necessarily hold true in all situations? Who was it that said at one time, "All that remains for the forces of evil to take over the world is for the good to do nothing"? Perplexing!* Obviously, the two axioms could not have been be formulated from the same point of view. From his long involvement in sports, he was accustomed to expect that those who did not observe the rules of fair play were penalized, disqualified, or thrown out of the game by the judges and umpires. Provided that their violations were discovered, of course! However, in this case, who was the referee, except God perhaps, he speculated. Anyway, for the present, these four hoodlums were still on the field, apparently invincible, and playing by their own set of rules. The forces of good?

I have to do something, he pressed on. He looked at the ropes tying his wrists and tried to pull his hands loose. The harder he tried, the deeper they dug into his skin.

Good God, the game is over. We have lost. I am trapped. I am caught in the spider's web . . . Such lousy sports!

* * *

Hank had trouble focusing his thinking. Everything had happened so quickly. One moment he had been enjoying a peaceful nap, and the next, he realized that he was tied to a tree for no apparent reason, and threatened to have his throat cut, if he caused any 'problems.' He shook his head trying to wake up, as if what had happened was a bad dream. No, it was not a dream. He could feel the ropes pressing his wrists firmly against tree branches. To his right, he could still see the tall stranger sitting on the boulder, observing the valley through Jack's binoculars. And through the branches, he could partly see two of the other strangers sitting next to the girls further up on the overlook. A fourth was sitting by himself at the other end drinking quietly from a bottle. Hank wondered who the men were. *What did they want and why did they do it?*

Gradually, his head cleared. He tried to establish eye contact with Jack, who was tied up to a tree on his left. But Jack appeared to be in deep thought, with his head bent forward on his chest. *Was he hurt?* An intense feeling of indignation began to flow through him. Lorie too had been manhandled, and a knife put to her back. *Good Lord Jesus! Those men are hardened criminals. What will they do next?*

Waves of anxiety rolled over him, and he felt his heart beating rapidly. He bowed his head and prayed for a long time for protection and deliverance, not only for himself, but for the other hikers as well. Still, he felt deeply humiliated by having been taken by complete surprise, and a feeling of shame and guilt came over him. At least Jack had shown some sign of manhood by ordering Lorie released and calling her attacker a 'scum.'

He wondered how Lorie would react to all the barbarism. She had always been so considerate and gentle, trusting, generous, and understanding. Could this remarkable woman, whom he loved dearly, cope with this terrible experience, or would her mind snap? He shuttered at the thought. Again, he looked through the branches and saw that Lorie had reclined herself on the overlook and her guard sitting next to her with a bottle in his hand and ogling her over. *He could not be thinking of . . . ?* No, the thought was too terrifying.

Subconsciously, he tried to work his hands free of the ropes, but without any result. *I feel so utterly impotent, so useless,* he groaned lowly between his teeth. *Why can't the law keep such individuals locked up so they won't abuse peaceful and decent citizens?*

Tears came trickling down his cheeks. He wanted to wipe them away, but his hands couldn't move.

* * *

"I have had enough, and it's probably time that we get back to the others. You are just too good, Howie. I concede." Eric sat down on the tree trunk and wiped the sweat off his forehead.

Howie threw his last two stones. They impacted squarely in the target area, which by now was dotted by many silvery gray spots, where the stones had hit. "That was a pretty good workout," he said, satisfied with his performance, and sat down next to Eric.

"Boy, isn't it nice here? I wish we could stay here for several days. Do you like it?" asked Eric.

"Yeah. But remember that we have a game against the 'Tigers' tomorrow evening. I wouldn't want to miss that. That's a must game for us."

"Right. I almost forgot that. If we win, the pennant is ours! We can do it, I am sure." Eric stood up. "Come, let's have a last cool drink of water and then get on our way."

Howie went in the lead as they returned the same way they had come. The sounds of splashing and running water faded out, and the stillness of the deep woods again surrounded them. The trail was now going steadily uphill, which required concentration and effort. When they came to the place that had been blocked by the spider's web, Howie stopped briefly to catch his breath. Without saying a word, he picked up a stick and slashed the web several times, so it came to hang in tatters on the tree trunks, and the path was open. The spider barely managed to escape to a tree branch, where it hid itself behind a piece of loose bark.

"Why did you do that?" asked Eric, surprised.

Howie looked puzzled. "No particular reason, but why not? Would you enjoy being caught in the web?"

"No, of course not. But even if I had been, I doubt that the spider would have been able to take advantage of me," replied Eric with a grin.

"Well, it might have stung you! Why take the chance?"

"I suppose that you are right, Howie. Hey, I have an idea!"

"Yeah?"

"Let's play we are Indians. You know, they used to hunt in these woods. Maybe we can come close to a squirrel or some other small animal. And when we get back to the overlook, we will surprise them by suddenly jumping in and shouting war cries!"

"Sounds like fun! Lead the way, Big Chief."

Bending down to a crouching position, Eric left the trail and twisted his way through the underbrush, trying to avoid making loud noises. Howie followed a few steps behind. At first it was most difficult without making long detours because of the steep and rocky terrain, but soon they learnt to pick the best route without losing direction. Several times, they stopped to watch field mice and squirrels scampering about. Gradually, the terrain leveled, and the sky again became visible through the branches.

Eric motioned to Howie to join him and asked in a whisper, "Tell me, Hawkeye, where is the enemy's camp?"

"Ugh, Big Chief, straight ahead, about a hundred paces," replied Howie, playing his role. "Why do I think so? Because the breeze is in my face, and I can smell the fireplace. Ha!"

"That's the way I read it. Let's sneak over behind that rock at the top and get ready for our attack!"

Quietly, they sneaked forward, maintaining the crouched position among the twisted trees and shrubs. They could now see the trail leading to the overlook on their left, and they felt a certain satisfaction in having been able to find their way without following the marked path.

Crouching to stay hidden from view behind the boulders and jagged rocks on the uphill side of the overlook, they covered the last distance and dropped down behind a large boulder.

"I think that we made it without being discovered by the palefaces, Hawkeye," whispered Eric. "Now, let's peek to see where they are." He raised his head high enough to get a view of the overlook.

His head came down again quickly. "Howie, it looks like something is wrong down there. Take a peek and tell me what you think."

* * *

Lorie startled as she felt a hand running through her hair. She opened her eyes and saw her guard's face next to hers. His blue eyes had a faraway expression, and his mouth was partly open. He had reclined close to her, supporting his head in his right hand. Once more, he brushed through her hair with his left hand. "You hair looks so pretty," he said admiringly.

"Don't . . . Don't! . . . For God's sake, don't do it!" Lorie felt her throat tighten, so she could barely whisper the words.

"Be quiet! Just be quiet as you were told, and you will be all right . . . Good girl, that's better." His hand went through her hair once again, continued around her neck, and stopped, holding her chin. His eyes rested on her lips, and he touched them with a finger.

She tried to speak or shout, but she wasn't able to get a sound out. Finally, in an effort to stop him, she tried to get up. Her guard's eyes suddenly assumed a hard expression as his hand pressed her head back and held it firmly against the hard ground. With his right hand, he pulled his knife from the sheath and pointed it at her throat, hissing angrily, "You damned bitch! Do you really want to get hurt? I'll kill you if you resist! Can't you understand that? Just play along. You understand?"

Feelings of terror and revulsion overpowered Lorie, and she thought that she was going to faint. Black spots floated in front of her eyes, and she had trouble breathing. Her mind faintly registered, *What kind of monster is he? He must be a disciple of the devil. What is God's purpose of letting me meet with this depraved individual?*

Apparently satisfied with the effect of his threat, the guard stuck the knife back in the sheath and reclined as before beside her. After a few minutes, he again began stroking her hair, neck, and lips.

In a semiconscious state, she felt him move closer, his warm and strong smelling body pressing against her left side. He buried his face in her hair, while his left arm came resting on her body as the fingers were playing on her lips. A voice in her mind kept echoing, *I will kill you if you resist! . . . I will kill you if you resist! . . .*

His breathing became faster and deeper, and he placed his left leg on top of hers. *That monster . . . that disciple of Satan! Is he going to violate me? . . . I will kill you if you resist! . . .*

Now breathing heavily, he pushed himself on top of her, alternately burying his face in her hair and kissing her forehead passionately. She felt her hands being pinned underneath his thighs as he planted his knees on both sides of her. Subconsciously, she pulled her hands free, and they came to rest on his leather belt. *I will kill you if . . .*

The man's right hand now began fondling her breasts. Her anguished thinking dissolved into meaningless fragments of sentences, *If you resist . . . Monster . . . I will kill . . . Satan . . . God's glory . . .* Her left hand moved to her assailant's hip and clutched the hilt of his knife, drawing it out from its sheath. *Devil . . . I will kill you if . . .*

She now felt the man's hand moving downwards from her breasts and beginning to fumble with the belt in her shorts. In a blinding flash of indignation and anger, she moved the knife up until its sharp point was aimed at the center of his back. The right hand came around to join the left in holding firmly the knife's hilt. *I will kill you if. . .* With all the strength of desperation, she forced the man's own knife into his back as deep as she was able to push it.

The blade entered about one inch to the left of the vertebra between the fifth and sixth rib, penetrating the muscle tissue, slicing the wind pipe, and spearing the heart's right ventricle. The man's heart immediately went into fibrillation.

She felt the hand moving away from her shorts, and the weight on her body lightened. When she opened her eyes, she saw that the man was trying to raise himself with both arms. His eyes were staring wide open, and his face was grimacing grotesquely in pain. He looked at her with a mixture of surprise and disbelief while groaning, "You bitch . . . you witch! I didn't know that you were . . . damn you . . . Go to hell! Owsch . . ." He rolled over, landing at her left side, coming to rest on his right shoulder while still facing her. His left arm, jerking in spasms, was still resting on her abdomen.

His bulging eyes and grimacing face was a horrible spectacle. Lorie lifted the man's arm away from her and rolled over on her right side to get him out of sight. She could still hear his rattling for several minutes. *What have I done? What's going to happen now?*

Her shoulders were heaving as she sobbed. She again folded her hands and prayed, "Heavenly Father, forgive me, for I have transgressed against thy holy commandment. I didn't know what else to do. Why did you send him here?"

* * *

Howie lowered himself to the ground beside Eric. He looked worried as he spoke. "I see four other people down there. It looks like they have tied your father and Mr. Wannamaker to some trees and they are guarding your mother and Mrs. Wannamaker. Right now, one of them is pointing a knife at your mother. My guess is that they are robbers. What else could they be?"

Eric buried his face in his hands. He felt like crying. When he was younger, it had always helped to cry when he was hurt, disappointed, or afraid, at which time his parents had tried to comfort him. But he understood that they could not help him this time. He was on his own! An almost irresistible urge to run away from the danger overcame him. But could he? Should he? And what about Howie?

Suddenly, he remembered what Mr. Wannamaker had taught them about the three ruling principles for their behavior when they were playing baseball: duty, valor, and fair play. It had been new words and ideas for most of the kids, but Mr. Wannamaker had patiently explained what they meant, and he insisted that they had to apply these three principles if they wanted to stay on the team.

That was it! I . . . we both have the duty to help free my parents and the Wannamakers from the robbers. We must show valor, meaning determination, courage, and imagination in the way we do it. What about fair play? Difficult! The robbers have knifes and are four against us two unarmed boys. Besides, they are holding hostages! An idea began forming in his mind, and he impetuously seized on it.

Howie was surprised by the sudden transformation in Eric's personality when he looked up again. Rather than looking confused and afraid as he did only a few seconds earlier, there was a new resoluteness in his face and authority in his voice. "Howie," he whispered, "do you remember duty, valor and fair play? This will be the test. This is what I think we ought to do. I will sneak around to free my father and Mr. Wannamaker. That will make it four against four. You will collect some rocks and a good stick. Stay on the high ground here. After I have finished freeing them, and we have collected some rocks ourselves, be ready to aim your rocks at the men guarding my mother and Mrs. Wannamaker. I will shout to my mother and Mrs. Wannamaker to stay down. When the men hear my voice, they will get up to look for me. Then we all will pelt them with rocks as hard as we can. We will have to hit them to make them go away, so we can free my mother and Mrs. Wannamaker. We will join you as soon as possible afterwards. Do you agree with my plan?"

"Gosh, Eric. Do you really think that will work? It sounds sort of freaky. What would happen if the robbers . . . ?"

But Eric cut Howie short. "Do you have a better plan?"

"Can't think of one! Other than wait here or maybe run for help."

"Help from whom? There is no one else here. We would have to go back to the highway for help. It would take many hours before the police would show up. The robbers may have killed my parents and the Wannamakers long before they arrived."

"Yeah. I see what you mean, Eric . . . Well, let's give it a try. You can count on me." Howie felt inspired by Eric's display of determination.

"Two things more, Howie. It has to be a surprise to work. Don't let the robbers discover you too early. And be ready to begin throwing as soon as we are organized!"

"I've got it."

"I knew I could count on you. Thanks, Howie." The boy's eyes met as they shook hands. Eric quickly turned and disappeared into the woods.

* * *

Noticing that her slumping guard was mentally light years away, Jill tried to keep up with Lorie's situation. It had not escaped her attention that Lorie's guard was showing a personal interest in his ward, and she began to fear for the consequences. At one time, she interrupted her own guard in his daydreaming and asked him to tell his friend to stop making advances towards Lorie. He had only responded gruffly, "Don't bug me, lady! Must I cut your throat to keep you quiet?" He hadn't even turned his head to see what she was talking about!

With growing anxiety, Jill had seen SS threatening Lorie once more with his knife. Jill covered her face with her hands and reflected, *Those individuals are true barbarians . . . mental derelicts.*

Why has society not locked them up in an asylum where they properly belong? My God, what can I do to help Lorie? This whole affair is going to end in tragedy . . .

When she looked again, SS was on top of Lorie groping her all over. Lorie was raising both of her arms behind his back. Was that a knife she was holding in her hands? Yes, it had to be the guard's own knife! Inside herself, she heard her heart shouting, *Do it, Lorie! Plunge it in. Give that scum what he deserves*! With exhilaration, she had seen the knife being pressed deep into the guard's back, followed by him rolling off Lorie in obvious pain. Jill was astonished to find herself thinking, *I hope that he is dying and will go straight to hell. They are well equipped to take care of cases like his.*

Now Jill was sitting next to her own guard, flushed and tense with emotion. She looked around and discovered to her surprise that she apparently had been the only witness to the execution. Everything seemed so utterly unreal. No one else was reacting. An eerie calm blanketed the overlook.

Jill tried to relax and analyze the new situation. She concluded that it was probably a change for the worse. If Lorie had in mind to try to escape now, she would have to join her, or else become the prime hostage. But would they be able to outrun the three remaining thugs in this difficult terrain? Very doubtful! And even if they were successful in escaping, Jack and Hank were still at the mercy of the thugs. In any event, judging from their previous demeanor, the thugs would probably crave a bloody revenge for their slain companion. The realization that they had probably moved from the ashes into the fire made her feel faint and clammy.

She was interrupted in her thinking by the sound of her guard stirring, and she turned to watch him. He was looking in the direction of Lorie and her guard. *He is bound to find out now!* she thought. *The moment of fury and revenge is about to begin.*

Her guard got clumsily on his feet to get a better look. After a moment, he called, "Hey, buddy, are you all right?" As no answer was heard, he walked a few steps towards his companion and repeated more loudly, "Are you awake, SS?"

* * *

Howie had finished collecting about two dozen rocks of suitable sizes and had arranged them into piles on a flat part of the boulder he was hiding behind. He had also found a sturdy stick, more than an inch in diameter and about seven feet long in the woods. He was about to place it beside the piles of rocks when he heard a voice from the overlook call out.

That must be the signal, he thought as he raised his head above the boulder. *Yes, one of the guards is standing up and looking around. But where is Eric?* He quickly took a rock in each hand, climbed up on the boulder, and got himself set for throwing.

The guard must have heard the noises from Howie's activities, for he immediately turned and looked up at him. Howie wasted no time. Taking aim at the guard's midsection, he threw the first rock as hard as he could. It impacted with a thud on his soft belly, making him double over and stagger backwards. With surprise, Howie saw him losing his balance after a few steps and fall backwards with a groan, landing squarely on his back in the fireplace!

Impatiently Howie waited for Mrs. Henderson's guard to get on his feet. However, there was no response from him. He just kept lying on the hard ground next to her, without showing movements!

* * *

For the past fifteen minutes, High Command had been absorbed in surveying the long stretch of highway in the valley. The traffic had been relatively light, and he didn't see any evidences of roadblocks or unusual activity by the highway police. At one time, he did observe a police car heading south at regular speed before disappearing from his view. With satisfaction, he concluded that so far, it appeared as if no concentrated effort was being made to locate the four of them.

He placed the binoculars beside him and slid down the boulder to stretch his legs. Surveying the overlook, he found that everyone was accounted for, and he walked back to his observation post and resumed his position on the boulder, alternatively thinking, keeping watch on the valley, and enjoying the content of his bottle.

He had just thrown the emptied bottle away from the bluff and heard it splinter far below, when he became aware of a loud groan and, a few seconds later, a wailing sound behind him. He turned around and realized that the sounds came from Firebird, who was lying on his back in the fireplace, with smoke beginning to rise from his clothes. Mesmerized, he watched him struggle in an effort to get back on his feet. At first he thought that it was one of Firebird's pranks, and a broad grin spread on his face.

High Command squinted his eyes to better see what was going on. The liquor had dulled his perceptions and slowed his reactions. He registered that Firebird now was on his feet staggering towards Crazy, who had been resting on the sloping part of the far end of the overlook, close to the outer rim, while staring empty into the sky. Approaching, Firebird shouted in agony, "Crazy, man, you've got to help me! My back is burning! Can't you put out the fire? Quick, help me!"

Crazy scrambled onto his feet. He was swaying, his arms hanging limp at his sides, and his dark eyes fixed on Firebird. "What is it you want?" he finally asked in a thick voice.

Firebird grabbed Crazy by the shoulders, shook him, and screamed into his face, "I am burning, man. Can't you see? Help me, I am hurting badly."

Crazy kept standing as if he was paralyzed and seemingly not comprehending what Firebird was saying. Then he tried to step away from Firebird, thereby placing himself higher than his friend, and with Firebird between himself and the rim of the overlook. However, Firebird kept holding on to his shoulders and screamed once more, "For crying out loud, man, do something! Don't just stand there! Put out the fire, Crazy! . . . Now!"

Confused, Crazy suddenly lifted his arms, grabbed Firebird's wrists, and tried to push him away while muttering, "Get your hands off me, Firebird. I've done you nothing!"

The sudden push, combined with the effect of the sloping rough ground and his lack of self-control, made Firebird lose his balance once more. He swayed back towards the yawning abyss behind him. In a desperate effort to recover his balance, he grabbed hold of Crazy's left wrist. However, Crazy was totally unprepared to resist the pull, as he was standing limp and with his feet close together. He was jerked one step forward before he also lost his balance and fell against Firebird.

The grin vanished abruptly from High Command's face as he watched his two companions linked together tumbling over the rim. Firebird kept holding on to Crazy's wrist as they were falling, and Crazy seemed peculiarly relaxed, obviously unaware of the disastrous consequence of his actions.

Three seconds later, High Command heard two almost simultaneous loud thuds, followed by several other bumps and the sounds of breaking branches. At last, he snapped out of his stupor, got off the boulder, and leaned over the rim get a last look of his two comrades, lying motionless and partly obscured at the base of the bluff.

* * *

Eric came out from the underbrush in a crouched posture and entered the area where his father was tied up. He unfolded the blade of his pocket knife, a recent gift from his parents on his fourteenth birthday. He touched his father's shoulder and whispered, "Dad, it's me, Eric. Please be quiet. I am going to cut your ropes. As soon as you can, pick up some rocks while I am freeing Mr. Wannamaker. We will have to drive the visitors away to get hold of Mom and Mrs. Wannamaker."

The quiet words registered through the confusion, anger, fear, and despair clouding Mr. Henderson's mind. He lifted his head and gave Eric a grateful look. However, while Eric was cutting his ropes, his attention was suddenly diverted by a penetrating wailing from the overlook. Turning his head, he watched the frantic efforts by one of the intruders apparently lying in the fireplace and trying to get out. Spellbound by the scene, he felt his ropes loosen and fall away.

The brooding Jack Wannamaker's attention had also been attracted by the wailing. He quickly surveyed the surroundings and discovered with surprise that Eric was close by, furiously cutting at his father's ropes. After that was completed, Eric came over and started to work on his ropes while whispering, "Collect some rocks quickly, and aim for the big man sitting on the boulder."

Animated, Jack sputtered, "I shall do that with the greatest of pleasure. I have a score to settle with that fellow. Thanks for coming, Eric." He rubbed his wrists to get the blood circulating and began collecting rocks.

* * *

At length, High Command, standing close to the place where his two friends had fallen off the overlook, concluded that they were gone forever. There was no hope that they could have survived the fall. His first thought was that the girl Firebird had been guarding had pushed him into the fireplace. With mounting rage, he stomped across the overlook towards Jill, who had not moved after Firebird had left her. He bellowed loudly, "I know that it was you who did it, you bitch! Did you not?' As he was shouting, he drew the knife from his belt.

As if hypnotized, Jill remained frozen, apparently unable to say or do anything. Drawing nearer, he lifted his arm with the knife, threatening, and spouted full of venom, "You damned whore! I will cut you to pieces for this!"

A rock came whistling towards High Command, hitting him hard on the left knee. Feeling the stinging pain, he looked surprised in the direction from where the rock had come and discovered a teenage boy standing on the top of a large boulder near the entrance to the overlook. He stopped to rub his knee and shouted towards SS, "SS, will you take care of that boy?"

High Command was less than ten feet away from Jill, who now seemed to have collected herself. She got up, looked High

Command in the eyes, and began lecturing him in a parental manner. "Mr. Leader, whatever your name is. Not only do you lack civility and objectivity, but you are foolishly getting yourself out on a very thin limb. Let me remind you that it was you who started this whole unpleasant series of events. As far as I am concerned, the sooner you disappear, the better." She then turned and went over to the hysterically sobbing girl next to SS, sat down next to her, and embraced her. High Command appeared to be flabbergasted when he saw that SS did not try to stop her.

Suddenly, a volley of rocks came at him from his right side, and more rocks were thrown by the boy at the entrance. Looking right, High Command now realized that the two men he had earlier tied to trees were advancing against him, joined by still another teenage boy he had not seen before. They all continued to throw rocks in his direction! He was hit by several!

* * *

Eric, his father, and Mr. Wannamaker had hastily been gathering rocks when they heard the leader's angry shouting and saw him walking towards Jill. Eric waved the two others forward, saying, "Let's spread out. We have to get him away before he gets hold of Mrs. Wannamaker!"

At about sixty feet distance, the leader was still out of effective throwing range. They scampered forward across the lose rubble while fanning away from each other. Had it not been for Howie's hit on the leader's knee, which delayed him, High Command would almost certainly have seized Jill before the three had come within throwing range. Those few lost seconds robbed him of a potential hostage and sealed his fate.

As soon as Jill had removed herself, Eric let his first rock fly and saw it grazing High Command's shoulder. Then Jack, driven by an inner fury, began to throw as fast as he could, and one of the rocks hit the man's right thigh hard, and another bounced off the side of his head. Advancing a little at a time, the three kept throwing at the man they had come to loathe, despise, and reject.

At the sight of the advancing threesome, the leader again shouted to Lorie's guard, "Get going, SS! Wake up! Get hold of the girls!" He then turned back facing his attackers, lifted his hand with the knife, and roared furiously, "If you throw one more rock, one of your girls will have her throat slit to the bone! Is that too difficult to understand?"

The attackers suddenly became uncertain and ceased their throwing, nervously glancing towards the girls. Eric, who sensed that something had gone wrong with the plan, shouted to Howie, who was still standing at the entrance, "Didn't you get him, Howie?"

Before he could answer, Lorie called back. "Don't worry about him. He is dead."

Hearing the answer, the outraged leader, who had been staring at his attackers with a transfixed, hateful gaze, snapped his head around to make certain that his only remaining ally had control of the girls. Only then did he realize that no help would be forthcoming from his accomplice, who was lying motionless on the ground. The leader's face turned pale. He turned and started to limp hurriedly back towards the big boulder he had been using earlier.

A cheer went up from the three stone throwers, who resumed advancing towards the retreating hoodlum, pelting him hard. In addition, Howie, with an armful of rocks, came down from the entrance and joined them in the assault at close range.

The leader was within an arm's length of the protective boulder when a rock hit him hard in the forehead. He dropped his knife and collapsed on the ground. The four attackers, encouraged by the turn of events and venting their emotions, began to jeer as they continued throwing several more rocks at their tormentor. "Here, have a taste of your own medicine." "What's the matter, bully? Can't you get on your throne?" "Why don't you go to your friends in hell?" or simply, "Good riddance."

The big man was lying still, bruised by many hits, and unconscious.

Jack Wannamaker shouted in a shrill tone of voice, "Throw the louse out," and took hold of an arm of the lifeless big man.

"Let him join his comrades," echoed Howie, taking the other arm.

Jointly, Jack and Howie began dragging High Command to the rim.

"Hey, wait a minute," called Hank Henderson, stopping them at the edge. "Don't you want to get back your wallet first, Jack?" He reached into the pocket of High Command's jeans, where his and Jack's wallets were kept. He handed Jack his wallet and stuck his own into a shirt pocket.

With Jack and Howie taking hold of High Command's arms and Hank and Eric holding on to the legs, they swung him back and forth several times before releasing him into the open space beyond the overlook, accompanied by their hooting and holloing. The big body sailed away from the overlook, spinning slowly in the air, and crashed into the underbrush below. The four embraced and shook hands in celebration of their delivery and victory.

* * *

Chapter 10

Backlash

"Thanks, fellows," exclaimed Jack Wannamaker, out of breath, and with emotion in his voice and tears in his eyes. "That was too close for me. Does anyone know what happened to the fourth of them? He seems to be out of it. Did you hit him, Howie?"

"No, I didn't, Mr. Wannamaker. He never got up. I saw that he has a knife in his back."

Together, they walked to where the women were sitting. The face of the hoodlum lying on the ground next to Lorie was twisted in a macabre grimace, and his piercing eyes were open and staring at her. Seeing Jack arriving, Jill looked up, "Poor Lorie. I think that she is in a state of shock."

Hank sat down and took Lorie tenderly in his arms. "Praise the Lord that you are still alive. Are you hurt, honey?"

Shaking all over, Lorie buried her face in Hank's shirt and threw her arms around him. Between sobs, she stammered, "Hank, I am a murderess! . . . I killed . . . him! I don't know why I did it, but I killed him . . ."

"Easy, honey, easy. This is all a terrible nightmare." Hank

motioned to the others to move the corpse of the guard away and leave them alone together.

The Wannamakers and the boys carried the corpse to the rim of the overlook. Jack was about to remove the knife from SS's back, but he changed his mind. Instead, he took a paper napkin from a pocket and wiped the knife's hilt. "I think that it is best for Lorie if she never sees that face again. Let's throw him down to the others," he whispered. Jointly, they lifted the dead man and threw him off the overlook.

* * *

Exhausted in body and mind, Jill and Jack sat down, leaning against the same boulder High Command had used for his survey of the valley. They held hands while trying to put the recent happenings in perspective.

After a pause, Jill asked, "How deep a cut did he give you?" She unbuttoned his shirt and inspected the wound on his chest.

"I don't think that it is anything serious. See, the blood has already dried up," replied Jack. He took the paper napkin from his pocket and tried to wipe the clotted blood away.

"Here, let me do it," insisted Jill. She took the napkin, wetted it with saliva, and rubbed the wound to dissolve the blood. "I don't think that it is more than a small puncture wound, but the gall of that man! Why did he do it?"

"He said that he was mad at me because I had called that guy that held Lorie a 'scum.' I suppose that he wanted to teach me a lesson in good manners and humility!"

"He was a madman, period! A complete maniac. Way out of control. I can't imagine what brought them up here on the mountain in the first place. They seemed to be so far out of character for nature lovers."

"I doubt if we will ever know. Let's be content that the whole sordid affair is over. You know, it was only fifty minutes ago they came barging in on us, but somehow I feel fifty years older now. I surely wish that it had never happened. How are the boys taking it?"

"Well, I think. They are sitting over there talking together. Why don't you close your eyes while I check on Lorie's condition?"

Jill rose and walked over to the Hendersons, dropping the blood-soiled napkin in the fireplace on the way. From the look on Hank's face, she understood that Lorie had not yet recovered from her ordeal. Holding his wife tightly, Hank again motioned that they wanted to be left alone. Jill then proceeded on to the two boys, who were squatting on the northeast end of the overlook.

"How is Mom, Mrs. Wannamaker?" asked Eric, looking worried.

"She is safe but still very frightened. Your dad is trying to calm her down. And how are our two heroes?"

"Fine. We are OK," Howie replied. "Actually, we were kind of scared too, wouldn't you say, Eric?"

"For sure."

"What you two did was very courageous. Tell me how you discovered that we were being held prisoners, and how you figured out a way to free us?"

Eagerly, the boys took turns telling what had transpired. "It was Eric's idea that I should stay up there while he freed you and Mrs. Henderson," finished Howie.

"The funny thing was that Howie thought that it was me who called, when it was your guard shouting to his dead friend. So Howie got up and started throwing long before we were ready," added Eric.

"It was a good plan anyway, and it all worked out for the best. Now, rest yourselves before we begin the hike down."

Jill returned to Jack and sat down. They heard someone yodeling expertly from somewhere in the mountains. "I believe that it is the same kind of yodeling we heard about an hour ago, but now it is much closer. They have good voices," commented Jack. "Well, is Lorie getting over it?"

"Lorie is still having a difficult time. I am beginning to wonder if she can make it down on her own."

"Lorie is a decent girl, who, I am sure, never has deliberately hurt another person before. It must have been a very traumatic event for her."

"I agree. Her standards are very high. The real question may be if she can forgive herself for what happened? Having killed a human being is a mortal sin by her definition and faith. I wouldn't be surprised if she can't stop blaming herself. She may have to live with that self-accusation. Tragic!"

Jack looked at his hands. "I must confess that neither am I particularly proud of what I participated in a little while ago. Let's face it, we behaved like a stone-age mob! I suspect that we all have a feeling of the same self-loathing deep down because of the way we behaved in this whole ghastly affair . . . No, it was not fair play. Our only excuse is that we were scared and felt humiliated and angry and that the situation was intolerable. You have no idea how scared I was when that big guy came after you with his knife drawn. I was convinced that he was about to use it on you."

"We were all scared, and no wonder," replied Jill. "But all that is water over the dam now. Let's instead think of how we are going to make it back to the car."

"It's ironic. We ought to be happy and celebrating. The troubles are over, and we lucked out. We are safe and free again without having been seriously hurt ourselves. The dragon is slain and gone for good. And yet there is no feeling of joy. Like Lorie, I suddenly feel that we have lost something precious in the process. Did we play by the rules? Yes, but not by our usual civilized rules! Instead, we stooped down to their barbarian rules, which at the moment seemed to be the only option we had to get out of the mess. But by doing so, didn't we become barbarians ourselves just like them? That's what's getting me down."

"It was an impossible choice," continued Jack, looking tired and unhappy. "Shakespeare had it right when he portrayed Hamlet's impossible choice three hundred years ago. 'To be or not to be?' How true. You are tossed between the sharp points of a dilemma. Once evil and mistrust enters the game, there is no way either team can win with honor! . . . I hope that at least the boys will be able to quickly forget what just happened."

"You are drained, Jack. Try to relax a little. Look at it this way: We are very fortunate that we came out of that episode unscathed!"

"Did we really? Did we not get smeared and depredated?" replied Jack with a sigh of resignation, closing his eyes.

* * *

Jill got up and began walking slowly around the overlook deep in thought. *Except for the kids, it seems that I am the least affected by the ordeal,* she reflected. *Someone has to take charge and get us back to the car and home.*

Her eyes fell on her guard's nearly empty bottle still standing on the ground where they had been sitting. She picked it up and studied it. *I suppose that I should thank you, bottle? Had it not been for you, your owner might still have been alive and holding me hostage. And what about your brother over there?* She walked over and took the bottle Lorie's guard had been drinking from. Studying that too, she continued her thinking, *I don't know about you. Did you make him do it? . . . No, of course not. You cannot do anything! You are not even empty!* She walked idly to the rim and threw both bottles away. *At any rate, you are no longer needed here. Join your owners.*

She drifted over to the large boulder from where the hoodlums' leader had been scouting the valley so intently. She climbed up and placed herself in the same spot where the leader had been sitting. *What might he have been looking for?* She took Jack's binoculars, which were still lying on top of the boulder, and put the strap around her neck. She looked through them and focused on the mountains and the valley, but that was hardly what had preoccupied the leader. He just didn't seem to have that kind of sensitivity. He must have been studying the highway below. Was he expecting something to happen down there? She did not see anything unusual. Just the normal traffic flow. And yet . . . The hawk they had seen earlier was back again, soaring gracefully back and forth above the bluff. What might have attracted the bird?

She suddenly became conscious of sitting in the same place

the leader had chosen just a short time before, and she felt uncomfortable and tense all over. She jumped off the boulder and walked up to the place at the trail entrance from where Howie had thrown the rock that caused her guard to tumble backwards into the fireplace. The tenseness would not leave, and her knees began shaking, feeling as if they were made from rubber. She sat down on another rock and continued the survey of the highway through the binoculars.

Deep in thought, she became aware of footsteps behind her, and she jumped up and called out nervously, "Who is there?"

"Good afternoon, my dear lady. We are sorry that we startled you. We didn't know that you were here. Please accept our apology for sneaking up so quietly. We are the Taylors. Would you mind if we join you for a while and share the view?"

The new arrivals were a couple. The man appeared to be about fifty years old, looking quite distinguished, even in his hiking outfit. His narrow face was highlighted by clear blue eyes and a narrow moustache. He was slender, walked with ease, and spoke with a clipped accent. His companion appeared to be considerably younger than he and had a smiling broad face framed by a mop of blond hair. She too was dressed for hiking, and Jill noticed that she was carrying a knapsack, whereas the man did not.

Seeing the unexpected strangers flustered Jill. Should she explain their situation and ask for help or not bring it up unless asked? After all, she thought, *we should be able to return on our own.* Why inconvenience them? She chose the latter course and forced herself to answer, "By all means. Make yourself at home."

Noticing Jill's tenseness, the Taylors exchanged glances. Mr. Taylor thanked her and added, "This is indeed a heavenly spot!"

Hearing those words, Jill thought with bitterness, *How can anyone say so after what has just happened here?* Involuntarily tears welled up in her eyes, and she hurriedly turned her head away.

"Did I say something rude?" asked Mr. Taylor with concern in his voice and looking at his companion.

Mrs. Taylor replied, "Not that I have heard, Liebchen." Her voice was warm and resonant.

Jill struggled to get hold of herself and finally managed to speak, "No, Mr. and Mrs. Taylor. It's just that . . . In fact I welcome you. It's good to see some normal people again."

"I don't quite understand," Mr. Taylor said with a puzzled expression. "Is anything the matter?"

Jill again looked at the couple, wiping her tears away with her hands. Absentmindedly, she stuttered, "It is just that . . . if you had arrived half an hour earlier . . . you too might have been part of a nightmare that happened here."

Mr. Taylor looked at Jill with compassion. "Would you mind telling us your name?"

"Why, yes. I am Jill . . . Jill Wannamaker. That's my husband sitting over there leaning on the boulder, his name is Jack. His name is Jack Wannamaker. The couple sitting together over there are the Hendersons, Hank and Lorie. The two boys are Eric and Howie. Eric is the son of the Hendersons."

"And what was the nightmare that took place here half an hour ago, Mrs. Henderson? That is, if you don't mind telling us about it?" asked Mr. Taylor.

"I am not sure that I have it all sorted out yet. So many things happened, ugly things! I think that we are all a little shell choked. We were having a picnic here on the overlook less than two hours ago. After we finished eating, the boys went away to see a spring. Then suddenly, four strange men surprised us . . ." Haltingly, Jill described the turn of events ending with the fate of the four intruders, whose bodies were now lying at the base of the bluff.

When she had finished, Mr. Taylor commented, "No wonder you are frightened and upset. But it sounds like you have been most fortunate in having come through the experience unhurt. I can't say that I feel sorry for your macabre visitors. And how are the others in your party taking it?"

Jill looked at the still-shaking Lorie, whom Hank was cuddling in his arms, looking very worried. "I believe that we still have some delayed reactions," was her evasive answer.

"You mean as the results of regrets, mental anguish, disillusions?" questioned Mr. Taylor.

"As I said, many ugly things happened. We are not in the habit of hurting and killing people. They are not pleasant events to look back on."

"No, of course not. We quite understand. Why don't you try to relax here for a little while? We should like to meet the rest of your party," Mr. Taylor answered as the two of them went down to the overlook.

* * *

"Mr. Wannamaker? May we disturb you?"

Jack opened his eyes and looked up. The couple standing in front of him looked unfamiliar but friendly. He got up from his sitting position and greeted them. "Do we know each other?" he asked.

"We have not been formally introduced," answered the man, shaking Jack's hand. "We are the Taylors. We just happened to come this way, and your wife told us about your unhappy encounter. Are you all right?"

"I think so, at least as well as can be hoped for. Thank you. A small scratch and a thunderous headache, Mr. Taylor. Other than that, I am as good as new."

Mrs. Taylor looked at the cut on his chest. "Is that a knife wound?"

"It is not deep," assured Jack. "One of our visitors insisted on writing his autograph on me."

Mrs. Taylor removed her knapsack and produced a first-aid kit from it. "This won't hurt," she said, soaking a ball of cotton in a clear fluid from a small bottle. She rubbed the wound and inspected it closely. "It's clean and superficial. It will heal up in a week or so. Are you sure that you have no other wounds?"

"Yes."

"Your wife told us that the four visitors fell or were thrown from the overlook. Could you perhaps show us where they landed?" asked Mr. Taylor.

"It's pretty overgrown down there, but we can take a look."

Jack led them to where the leader had been thrown out. "The biggest of them should be somewhere in this general area," he said while pointing down. It took them several minutes before they were able to locate the barely visible body.

"Does he have anything on him that belongs to any of you?" asked Mr. Taylor.

"He did take our wallets, but we recovered them before we threw him out. Other than that, I can't think of anything!"

"Good," smiled Mr. Taylor. "Let's see if we can locate the other men."

They went to the place where Lorie's guard had been ejected and tried to locate his resting place. However, the search was futile, and they finally had to accept that no part of him could be seen from the overlook. The dense undergrowth appeared to have swallowed him up.

Mr. Taylor asked again if any of the intruders had anything on them which belonged to, or could be linked to Mr. Wannamaker's group.

Jack thought for a moment. "Not that I know of, except perhaps for the knife of Lorie's guard. Lorie had held it in her hands, and I touched it briefly later. I am not sure that I understand your question, sir? But, yes, I remember that I left the knife where I found it in the guard's back, and for some reason, I decided to wipe the hilt clean before we threw the body out. I have no idea why I did it, except perhaps that I was trying to protect Lorie? Well, the other two fell down together from the far end of the overlook."

They walked over to the place and looked down. Almost immediately, Jack discovered their outlines, and he pointed them out to the Taylors. "There they are, the poor devils. Lying within a few feet of each other."

The two boys, who had been sitting close by, came over to watch.

"Hey, be careful, Eric and Howie, unless you want to join the two down there. It's pretty steep here. Would you like to meet Mr. and Mrs. Taylor who just arrived?" asked Jack Wannamaker.

The boys nodded politely to the Taylors.

Mr. Taylor addressed the boys, "I understand that you boys acted most courageously?"

"We just did our duty, sir," Eric replied modestly.

"You mean freeing your parents and their friends when you saw that they were being held by those strangers? I would say that takes plenty of courage. Lots! I wonder who taught you that," continued Mr. Taylor.

"Mostly Mr. Wannamaker," Howie answered. "He is our baseball coach. Our team's ruling principles are duty, valor, and fair play."

Jack Wannamaker looked satisfied at the boys and said with a suppressed smile, "We all thank you for what you did today. Had it not been for your quick thinking and action, the four of us may very well have been hurt or liquidated in retaliation for the stabbing of Eric's mother's guard. On the other hand, don't get the notion that what we did collectively was fair play. It was barbaric and demeaning. Heroic? Perhaps. Civilized? Definitely not. I hope that none of us will ever be forced into a situation like this again and that, at least, you boys will be able to forget what transpired here. Eric, I believe that your mother is still in a state of shock. Let's go over and see if there is anything we can do to make it easier for her."

Together, the five walked over to Hank and Lorie. Hank looked up with a worried expression. "I don't know what to do," he whispered. "I have never seen her like this before. She just keeps crying and blaming herself for having done away with that beast. I hope that she is not losing her mind." His voice trailed into a sob.

Mrs. Taylor took a small bottle from her knapsack, unscrewed the cap, and handed it to Jack. "Here," she said, "try to make her drink some of this."

Hank rejected the offer, saying, "Neither of us drinks strong liquors."

Mrs. Taylor persisted, "Don't you worry. This is not a strong liquor. It's medicine that will calm your wife down."

Reluctantly Hank took the bottle and put it to Lorie's lips. "Sweetheart, drink some of this. It will make you feel better."

Between sobs, Lorie managed to swallow a little of the content of the bottle. Hank passed the bottle back to Mrs. Taylor, "Thank you very much."

Jill had come down from the entrance to watch Lorie's progress. Lorie's sobbing gradually diminished, and Hank said, with a glimmer of hope in his voice, "Sweetheart, it's going to be all right."

Lorie looked at her husband with a peculiar far-away expression. "Hank, can't you understand that it is not going to be all right? I have killed . . . we have killed! Our souls will be going straight to hell!"

"Please, don't say that, sweetheart. I can't bear it. I can't. Oh, Savior, protect us. Tell us what to do. Tell me, oh, Savior." Hank's composure disintegrated, and he started to weep hysterically.

Mrs. Taylor again handed the small bottle to Hank and asked him to drink some of the content. Without thinking, he emptied the bottle.

Visibly shaken by the whole scene, Mr. and Mrs. Taylor separated themselves from the group.

* * *

Jack and Jill took the boys with them and walked back to the large boulder. Once more, they wanted to give Hank and Lorie an opportunity to compose themselves in solitude. Eric, in particular, was very upset after having watched the agony of his parents. To make the boys think of other things, Jack took his accordion and played some old folk songs, without anyone singing. During an intermission, the Taylors came back to join them.

Mr. Taylor asked, "What are your plans now?"

"We hope that Hank and Lorie will recover enough before long, so we will be able to hike back to the parking lot before it turns dark," Jack replied.

"And if they don't?"

"That could be a real problem. It will probably start raining by evening, and there is no shelter nearby. We may try and carry them down, but that would be an almost impossible task, especially after it starts raining."

"Mr. and Mrs. Wannamaker, I know that this may sound strange to you, but I might be able to speed up the recovery time for Eric's parents so that you all can leave within an hour. However, if you want me to do so, it would take some cooperation from all of you," explained Mr. Taylor.

"If that were possible, we would be more than happy to assist in any way we can, but what are we to do?" asked Jill.

"My evaluation is that Mr. and Mrs. Henderson have been forced by external circumstances to behave in ways that are contrary to some of their deepest held principles and basic values. Now that the danger has passed, they are condemning themselves for the actions they took to defend themselves. Incidentally, some of the rest of you may have a degree of the same feeling of self-reproach? My wife and I think that we know of a way that will make them forget this whole horrid affair. However, to make it work for the Hendersons, it would be necessary for all of you to participate, to ensure that they would not hear any future accidental references from you about what did happen. Were they to be reminded later, it could easily result in a recall."

"How is that possible, Mr. Taylor? Are you a psychiatrist?"

"Not exactly, but I do have a fair amount of experience with the subject. Yes, I believe that it is possible. However, it would be an experiment, and I cannot guarantee the long range outcome. But, if everyone is willing, I shall do my best."

"I see no downside to what you are proposing," replied Jack. "I, for one, have no desire to remember our meeting with those barbarians. In fact, I should be eternally grateful if it had never happened."

"So would I," agreed Jill. "Please, Mr. Taylor, if you are serious, do whatever you can!"

"And what about you, young gentlemen?"

"I just want to see Mom and Dad happy again. I will do whatever is necessary," replied Eric.

"You can count me in too," echoed Howie.

"It won't take long," Mr. Taylor went on, "But there are a few things we must take care of first. Mr. Wannamaker, you said that there is nothing on the four dead men that can link them with your group?"

"Yes, I am sure of that."

"Second, did the four intruders leave any articles here on the overlook that could remind you of them."

They all looked around, and Jill said, "I threw their bottles away, but their jackets are still here. All four of them."

"And the leader's knife is still lying where he dropped it," added Jack.

"Has any of you touched that knife?"

Everyone denied so doing.

"Can you think of any other items," Mr. Taylor went on.

"No, that should sum it up."

"Very well. Please, don't touch any of those items. Then thirdly, is there any kind of creature common to this region that you dislike in particular?"

"Spiders!" Howie was quick to mention.

"Yeah, spiders are bad," affirmed Eric.

"That would seem to be a good choice," accepted Mr. Taylor. "We should be ready now. Would all of you please move over close to Eric's parents and arrange yourselves within hearing distance. Don't say anything. Just try to be quiet and relax. We shall be joining you in a minute."

While the four went over to Hank and Lorie, Mr. Taylor picked up the leader's knife using his handkerchief and threw it into the abyss outside the overlook. Mrs. Taylor collected the four black vinyl jackets and placed them in a pile on the ground next to the group.

* * *

Chapter 11

The Grand Experiment

When the Taylors returned, the Wannamakers and the boys had placed themselves on the ground close to Hank and Lorie, who had finally stopped sobbing. Mr. Taylor began speaking to them with a calm reassuring voice.

"Please make yourselves as comfortable as you can and look at me. Try to relax completely, especially you, Mr. and Mrs. Henderson. We understand that you have been through some very bad moments, but all that is behind you now and you are safe and already feeling much better. I am your friend, and I will watch over you. Nothing bad can happen now. Just relax and enjoy the peace that is coming over your mind." Mr. Taylor looked slowly from face to face, meeting their gazes.

"Yes, it is now very comfortable here, your minds are relaxed and at peace, and you are beginning to feel drowsy. Your eyelids are feeling heavy . . . very heavy . . . they want to close. You feel a wonderful peace surrounding you . . . nothing is disturbing, all is peace . . . peace. Your eyelids are closing shut now, but you can still hear my voice. There are no other sounds to hear than the words I am saying. Please keep listening to my voice."

One by one, the six pairs of eyes, watching him, closed. The faces were relaxed, and the heads tilted forward.

Mr. Taylor continued, "Please keep listening to my voice. You don't remember who we are, as you have never seen us before. What you are hearing are the sounds of the wind. You cannot see the wind, but the wind is speaking to you. Please listen carefully to what it says. You remember clearly that you hiked up the mountain to this overlook earlier today. You arrived at the overlook and had a pleasant picnic together. Now the picnic is over, and you are all having a rest. Nothing else has happened after you finished the picnic, except that you saw four spiders on the overlook coming crawling towards you. There they are! Don't be afraid of them, because they will not harm you. The wind is getting stronger and will now blow the spiders away from the overlook, blowing them far away, to a distant place, one by one . . . forever . . . and ever, while you are resting safely."

Mr. Taylor went over to the place where the four black vinyl jackets were lying, picked one of them up, and carried it to the rim of the overlook. Lifting it up over his head, he released it, and it was caught by the breeze and fluttered out of view from the overlook as he was saying, "This is the first spider to be blown far away." He went back to the pile and picked up a second jacket, which he handled in the same way, quoting, "This is the second spider to be blown far away." He repeated the procedure with the remaining two jackets, finishing the disappearances by saying, "This is the fourth spider to be blown far away. All four spiders have now been carried away by the wind, and you will never see them again." He returned to the group.

In his calm, reassuring voice, he continued, "As you know, the four spiders made a brief visit and then disappeared from the overlook. You are resting comfortably, feeling relaxed and safe. You will never again meet with those four spiders. Now, please go back in your memory and see if you can find any other events that has taken place after you finished your picnic. If you find any, take the first one that comes to your mind and tell yourself that you wish to forget all about it, as if it had never happened. It is now expelled from your memory. Please continue going back in your memory in the same manner, and if you find any other events that seem to have taken place after your picnic, expel them one by one until you are certain that there is nothing else that has happened. Keep searching . . . keep searching until you cannot think of anything else that has taken place after your picnic, except the arrival and departure of the four spiders and that you are having a good rest."

For several minutes, there was complete silence. Mr. Taylor continued in the same tone of voice. "You have been hiking up the mountain to this overlook. You had a pleasant picnic on the overlook. After you finished the picnic, you saw four spiders, but they are gone now. You are all having a comfortable rest. If you can think of anything else that has happened after the picnic, please nod your head."

No one's head nodded.

Mr. Taylor went on. "I have nothing further to say, except that in a short while, you will hear yodeling from the entrance to the overlook. When that happens, you will open your eyes, and you will all feel wonderfully refreshed and at ease. You will also feel a special joy in your hearts. You have not met with the yodelers before, but you will invite them to join your party. In half an hour, you will decide that it is time to leave the overlook and head home."

Mrs. Taylor had strapped her knapsack back on, and together, the Taylors left the group and ascended to the trail entrance. Standing there, facing the valley, the two began a melodic yodeling duet. "Yodle-ah-ei-du . . ."

At the first series of notes, the six reclining people on the overlook opened their eyes and began stirring.

"Do you hear those voices?" exclaimed Jack, looking at Jill. "They are absolutely fantastic!"

"They are. I have always enjoyed listening to yodelers. Not that I am any good at it, but those people know what they are doing. See, they are standing right up there," replied Jill, pointing to the entrance. "Should we invite them to join us?"

"That's a good idea, but let's wait until they have finished the yodeling."

Hank was stretching himself and looked at Lorie. "Boy, that was a delicious lunch you made for us. Say, I must have dozed off. And you too?"

"We all did, I think. It must have been all that hiking and the fresh air," replied Lorie, looking up at the trail entrance. "Look at who is coming. That's what I call a grand entrance!"

Howie touched Jack's shoulder, "They are cool! Can you do a number like that on your accordion?"

Jack grinned. "Not nearly as well, I am afraid. But I am willing to try a cheap imitation." He unpacked his accordion and strapped it to his shoulders. Just as the couple at the entrance were about to finish their yodeling, he joined them in the proper key and played their last theme over several times before developing it into an energetic polka with variations on most of the themes they had used, and with progressive use of bass and volume.

The two visitors laughed at Jack's showmanship and began clapping their hands in time to the music as they descended the rocks. Once down on the overlook, they began dancing together in time to Jack's music, which was no easy task, given the roughness and the scattered gravel and rocks on the overlook. But somehow, they managed dancing in a style so elegant that all available hands soon began to clap in time with their intricate steps.

Finally, Jack finished playing, and the two guests joined in the clapping of hands and exclaimed, "Bravo, bravo. You certainly know how to play the accordion." They sat down on a boulder to catch their breaths. "If you had played one more verse, we should probably have fainted. After a long hike, dancing a polka will surely wear you down."

"I was just trying to imitate your yodeling that inspired me. By the way, in case you are willing to give yodeling lessons, I should like to sign up immediately. That was a superb performance! May I introduce you to my family and friends. I am Jack Wannamaker . . ." He went on to introducing the rest of the group.

"We are the Taylors," answered the man. "We are pleased to have made your acquaintance."

"Honest, your performance or, should I say, performances were brilliant," exclaimed Lorie admiringly.

"Thank you very much, but we were just enjoying ourselves," replied Mrs. Taylor.

"Would you care to join us? How about some iced tea or an apple?" asked Lorie.

"An apple would be refreshing after all that hiking," accepted Mrs. Taylor.

"Indeed, an apple is just what I need," echoed Mr. Taylor.

Jill found some juicy apples in the knapsack, and Jack, who still had the accordion strapped on, suggested, "The boys have asked me if I would play a few tunes for them. If anybody feels like singing, don't be bashful. Perhaps we could even persuade the excellent voices of Mr. and Mrs. Taylor to join us? How about it?"

The Taylors shrugged their shoulders and looked at each other. "We can try! That's a great idea!"

With Jack playing, everyone joined in the singing of "A Happy Wanderer Am I."

* * *

About half an hour after the Taylors had shown up, Jack looked at his watch and let the air out of the accordion. "I hate to be the first to end the party, but we really should be thinking about getting on our way down. As you can see, the clouds are building up pretty fast, and the weather forecast is for rain beginning by evening."

"Shoot! I was just getting warmed up," complained Hank loudly. "But you are right! These trails probably will become mighty slippery once they get wet. Mr. and Mrs. Taylor, which way are you going?"

"Our car is parked where Route 184 runs into 105."

"How fortunate! That's where I parked mine. Would you like to stay with us on the way down? If so, we might even have a little sing-along as we hike?"

"That would suit us just fine, thank you."

"It's all set then. Everybody, break camp. Get your stuff together and ready to leave," shouted Hank.

* * *

The single file caravan of the eight hikers snaked their way along the narrow trail down from the Watauga Overlook. In the fading light under the overcast sky, the leafy tree canopy above them now was almost olive colored. The glittering garlands of dew they had observed on the stalks and grasses in the morning had long since evaporated, and the birds seemed to have flown elsewhere. However, their spirits were high, and they exchanged light hearted observations and jokes.

As they passed the camp ground on the knoll at the end of the blue trail, they encountered two young men with knapsacks sitting on a boulder on the opposite side of the knoll. One of them had what appeared to be a folded tent strapped to his knapsack, and they both were carrying rolled-up sleeping bags.

Jack waved to them shouting, "Are you going to camp here for the night?"

They returned the greeting and shouted back, "No, we are just passing through. We are heading south towards Grandfather Mountain."

"Then have a good trek," Jack shouted back.

After about an hour's hiking, the trail passed by an open shallow cave embedded under a large protruding rock, and they made a rest stop. Jack was passing apples around as Jill noticed some blood oozing out on his sweaty chest, just above the shirt opening. She brought it matter-of-factly to his attention, "Jack, your chest is bleeding."

Jack looked down. "Yes, I can see it. I must have scratched it on a branch or something. It does sting a little."

Mrs. Taylor brought out her first aid kit and insisted on treating the wound. With a wad of cotton, she rubbed it carefully with alcohol and covered it with a Band-Aid. "It will heal up nicely," she told him with a smile.

"Thank you, Mrs. Taylor," he responded. "Could I perhaps ask you for another favor? Your yodeling on the overlook still intrigues me. I wonder if the two of you would mind giving us an encore?"

The Taylors conferred with each other. "With pleasure,"

answered Mr. Taylor. "But you must know that there are no echoes in this particular place. The trees will muffle any sounds we make. To yodel well, there must be strong echoes. So the rest of you will have to provide the background."

"We will do our best if you will tell us how," replied Jack.

"Do you know how to whistle?" asked Mr. Taylor.

They all confirmed that they thought so.

"Let me hear you whistle 'Mack the Knife'!"

A few of the group began to whistle the tune, and before long, everybody had joined in. The chorus gained strength, harmonizing well, and keeping good timing.

"Excellent. That's just what we will need," said Mr. Taylor pleased. "If you will all start on three, my wife and I will join you in yodeling. Whistle the tune three times. The first time as a vigorous march, then slowly and softly, and finally, as if it were an energetic dance. Ready? One, two, three . . ."

With the rest whistling the familiar tune, the Taylors exhibited a masterpiece of yodeling. Beginning as a duet, they changed to solos, racing up and down the scales, weaving around the beat of the whistling. During the second verse, Mr. Taylor followed the beat of the whistlers, while Mrs. Taylor acted as his echo off the beat. And finally, during the third verse, they yodeled together in harmony, very simple and exquisite.

"Bravo, bravo! Encore."

"I don't want to dampen your enthusiasm, but I think that it's beginning to rain. Isn't that rain drops I hear hitting the leaves? We better get on our way," cautioned Mr. Taylor.

* * *

During the last half hour of the hike down, it rained intermittently. At first it was only some few scattered drops, which mostly were retained in the leafy canopy above. But gradually, the rain became more intense, and soon the leaves were water logged. The accumulated rain mist combined and fell off the leaves in oversized drops. The rain gear had to be unpacked. Wearing their raincoats and hats, the group was finally approaching the end of the trail.

By now, the sloping footpath had turned into a virtual shallow brook, and it became slippery, as water was absorbed into the ground. Even the carefully designed cleats on their hiking shoes could not prevent them from repeatedly losing their balance on many sections

Eric shouted to his father, who was walking in the lead, "Dad, I keep sliding. Can't we stop?"

Hank stopped and looked back. "I am not so sure that's a good idea, son. The trail is getting worse by the minute, and I estimate that we are within five minutes of the parking lot. Won't you be able to last that long, Eric?"

"My shoes are wet inside. They are heavy and full of mud," complained Howie.

With an unperturbed air, Mr. Taylor took charge by proposing, "I think that it may be time we get off the trail. That should make it easier for everyone. Please follow me." He stepped onto the uphill side off the trail and began picking his way between trees and shrubs and somehow managed to find more solid ground to walk on.

"Why didn't I think of that?" grumbled Hank.

Mr. Taylor began to whistle "Mack the Knife" and was joined by his wife. Before long, everybody was whistling as loudly as they could, as if they were no longer paying attention to the rain and their discomfort.

They were still whistling as they arrived at the wooden stairs to the parking lot. On their way down the stairs, they noticed that a police car was parked close to the road at one end of the clearing. Two uniformed men stepped out of the car and headed towards them. One of them talked to Jack for a few minutes, and Howie, who stood nearby, also exchanged a few words with the other.

The rest of the group, waiting impatiently in the rain, asked Jack what the discussion was about.

"They are looking for some missing people and asked if we perchance had met with them during our hike," answered Jack.

"They also wanted to warn us that the highways are getting very slick, so we better drive carefully. Well, Mr. and Mrs. Taylor, I am very reluctant to part ways with you, but I suppose that this is the end of our partying. It was a privilege to meet with both of you, and we have certainly enjoyed your company. I am still infatuated by your yodeling. That was really great stuff! Thanks for everything, and enjoy your vacation."

"We are glad it worked out so well. We had a good time too. It was a pleasure spending time with all six of you. Take care."

Mr. and Mrs. Taylor went to their car. A minute later, they pulled out onto the highway and drove northwards in the pouring rain.

Hurriedly, the remaining six loaded the Hendersons' station wagon with their knapsacks and the dripping rain gear and dived into the seats. As they pulled out of the parking lot, Hank resumed the conversation, "A soft seat out of the rain surely feels good after all that hiking!"

Lorie commented merrily, "Except for the rain, it really has been a marvelous day. Let's do it again soon."

Jack said, addressed to Jill, "Aren't they interesting and talented people, the Taylors? It's so uplifting when you meet people such as them."

"Yes, they are. I wonder what profession he is in. You know, I should have asked them. They were good enough to be some kind of entertainers."

Howie suddenly poked Eric in the side. "Hey, how come you never showed me that spring coming out of the mountain you talked so much about on the way up here?"

Eric commented dryly, looking through the window at the rain and clouds completely enveloping the mountains, "Yeah? And what do you call all that?"

* * *

Chapter 12

Good Samaritans

When Bobby McClure had finished his summary of the Henderson party's hike to the Watauga Overlook, the other guests were beginning to leave their tables. The band was still playing soft dancing music, and a few couples occupied the dancing floor. Stafford and Helen, however, had excused themselves and left for their room, not without being gently chided by the others for their 'early' departure.

McClure looked almost apologetically at Gretchen. "I hope that I did not go into too many details in this rather long explanation. You asked me if we, the law enforcement officers, always apprehended the criminals and brought them to a proper trial by the courts. I have tried to show, by using one example, that sometimes it is well neigh impossible to be sure that the justice of the law has been metered out."

Gretchen looked curiously at McClure and said, "Mr. McClure, thank you very much for your patience in trying to make us understand this very convoluted and, I must say, interesting case. I think that I now better understand the many practical difficulties you sometimes are up against. But, being totally honest, don't you agree that whether the grand jury was entirely correct or not, or whether all the events and circumstances included in your description actually were present, justice already has been done. In my view, you found and caught the criminals, even though they were dead at that time. I cannot imagine that any court could have sentenced them to a harsher punishment."

"Permit me to say that it is not as simple as that, Mrs. Schneider," answered McClure. "In theory, the law is supposed to be infallible. We, the four of us, may agree among ourselves that the perpetrators of the injuries to Ipsen and Tatum were amply punished, albeit not by any judicial court. Whether the hoodlums killed each other or fell or jumped off the bluff, they were already dead when we found them, and the law cannot prosecute any deceased person. But technically, if any of the four motorcyclists had been a victim of assault by outsiders, the law enforcement agencies are obligated to prosecute those who participated in the assault, of course, provided that they are still living, even if those persons may have acted in what they themselves considered to be self defense."

Ann, who had been silent for a long time, interjected with a long sigh, "I agree with Mrs. Schneider. Even if the events Bobby just hinted at could be proven to be factual, justice would still have been done as equitably as could be reasonably expected. It would have been an unnecessary, punishing ordeal for the six hikers to go through all the inquiries, court hearings, waiting times, uncertainties, and what not, and to have all the details reported in the newspapers and on the television. Their family life and their whole future would have been damaged, and they would probably never be able to forget the ordeal they went through for as long as they lived."

Bobby looked at Ann with a stiff, determined smile. "I do respect your opinion, Ann. All I am saying is that technically several additional crimes might have been committed, and, if so, that the perpetrators of those were not brought to trial by the judicial court, which, as you know, is one of the responsibilities of my department."

Gretchen cut in again, "Then please clarify for us if, in your judgment, the Taylors were implicated in the deaths of the motorcyclists?"

McClure scratched his head and answered with some hesitation, "Not directly, of course. But if there were any evidence that they had acted in the way I just mentioned, I suppose that a clever prosecutor could make indictments against them too on several counts, such as being accomplices and accessories to murder, removing or tampering with evidence from a scene of a crime, failure to report and testify, leaving a scene of crime, obstruction of justice, to mention just a few." His eyes studied Mr. and Mrs. Schneider attentively.

Ann broke the ensuing embarrassing pause with her laughter and looked with an amused expression at her husband. "Bobby, please come to your senses! In all the years I have known you, this is the most concocted explanation I have heard. Not only is it speculative and far fetched, but it is downright incredible. Excuse me for saying so, but my knowledge of human nature tells me that if anyone had mastered a feat like what the Taylors supposedly did in your tale, they would have been more than eager to broadcast to the whole world what happened. And apart from that, the good book does not say anything about the Good Samaritan calling the constabulary telling them: 'This poor fellow was robbed and beaten. Go and find the robbers so that they can be punished.' Especially, I would think, if he knew that the robbers already were dead. Forgive me, Bobby, I know that you are a good man yourself. Why can't you accept that the court already has made its just and fair verdict and that the case has been be closed for good?"

Bobby looked at Ann with a puzzled, and yet loving glance. After a few moments, he answered with a wry smile. "Sometimes I have difficulties understanding your reasoning, Ann. But this much I am certain of: You always want the best for everyone, and you firmly believe that 'Noblesse oblige' is more important than being right. Please remember, though, as I spelled out earlier, that what I laid out is only a previously untested hypothesis which, in my opinion, should not have been overlooked by us and the court. I suppose that I am not as eloquent in quoting books as you are, but

I do remember another quote, I believe from a famous English playwright that goes something like this: 'There is more between heaven and earth than you have ever imagined.'"

Bobby McClure twirled his now-empty glass between his fingers and added reflectively, "Frankly, to me, that hypothesis does not sound all that absurd, excepting perhaps for this one detail: Why did the Taylors inject the memory of four spiders having shown up on the overlook, only to disappear shortly later in the minds of the hikers? All six remembered this seemingly unimportant episode in exact identical details, without the slightest deviation, which is unheard of when many witnesses testify about the same event! Mr. Fontini, I believe that you mentioned earlier that you have studied psychology at the University of Vienna? I wonder if you can think of an explanation or may have a guess as to why?"

Mr. Fontini looked thoughtful for a long moment and then replied, "Yes, I did study psychology at the University of Vienna. But didn't I also mention that I never finished my studies, and I certainly didn't obtain a degree. And, as it is your hypothesis, I should think that your explanation would be as good or even better than any I can come up with."

McClure showed the faintest sign of being disappointed, but immediately stopped frowning. "Well, neither do I have a degree in psychology. What little I know about the subject is what I have managed to put together during many years of on-the-job training. To me, Howie's initial casual statement of having seen four spiders during the hike at first seemed irrelevant. But, finding out later that everyone in the party remembered such a minute detail is making me realize now that it could have been a clever ploy by Mr. Taylor in the event the memory erasing had been less than a complete success. As I see it, it would not be unreasonable to expect that any possible residue in the memories of the hiking party pertaining to their dealings with the four criminals, such as feelings of fear, intimidation, disgust, hostility, and so on, even unconsciously in their dreams, would be assimilated with the same negative feelings they had against the imaginary spiders, which fortunately, as everyone were convinced of, had been disposed of, and thus no longer were a cause for real concern. In other words, the spiders were conceived of as backup psychological scapegoats. Would you agree with such an appraisal, Mr. Fontini?"

"You certainly make it sound very plausible," Mr. Fontini replied amiably. "Indeed, you are most persuasive! I can't think of a better explanation myself."

"Well, at any rate, so much for my new hypothesis. Once more, I have tried to uncover what's hidden under this perplexing enigma, and I hope that you at least have found my effort entertaining, even if Ann thinks that the result is incredible," concluded McClure.

Mr. Fontini commented, "I must admit that you held us spellbound with your revaluation of this old case. All told, I thought that you did very well, whether you are right or not. May I ask, how are the two patrolmen, Ipsen and Tatum, doing now? And what has become of the Wannamakers and the Hendersons?"

"The last time I heard about them was about a year ago. I happened to run into Hank Henderson at a party fundraising meeting in Hickory. He has gained a little weight but otherwise seems to be in good shape. He said that his business was doing well. His wife is busy in their church and civic groups. Both Eric and Howie had recently graduated from North Carolina State University, both with an engineering degree. Hank also told me that Jack Wannamaker had been promoted to assistant principal at the high school. By the way, the Wannamakers now have two toddlers, a boy and a girl, and Jill has, at least for the foreseeable time, decided to devote her full time to their upbringing."

"That is wonderful! So Ipsen is the only one that still suffers disabilities?" queried Mr. Fontini. "Is he still with your department?"

"Yes. He is an asset, conscientious, dependable, and bright. His only remaining problems are these occasional dizziness spells and a slightly reduced sight on his right eye. So I am afraid that he will primarily remain assigned to office duty."

"How unfortunate, both for him and for his family! Mrs. McClure suggested earlier that memory erasing might alleviate the dizziness and the eye focusing problems. I hope that you understand that the probability of a cure by using such a treatment is not very high in his case. However, if you and Ipsen decide to go through with it, I shall be happy to try it out. At any rate, a good vacation in Austria may do the Ipsens some good. Send us a letter, if you decide to go ahead."

"You have no idea how much your offer means to me—to us. We will let you know in the near future."

Ann took Bobby by his arm and said, "Now I have five good reasons for taking you up to our room."

"Are any of them persuasive?" teased Bobby.

"First, my biological clock tells me that it is five in the morning. Second, the place is about to close. Thirdly, you are beginning to speak in hyperbolas. Fourthly, you are insulting the intelligences of Mr. and Mrs. Schneider. And fifthly, this is our silver anniversary wedding night," joked Ann.

Bobby threw up his hands. "True on every count, although I favor the last one as the most persuasive." Turning to the Fontinis, he continued, "I suppose that even magicians and illusionists need sleep once in a while? If you will excuse us, we would like to thank both of you for your kindnesses in making our silver anniversary party an event we shall always remember. It was a pleasure making your acquaintances, and we sincerely hope that there will be an opportunity to meet with you again."

"The pleasure was entirely ours, Mr. and Mrs. McClure. We wish you a pleasant vacation, a good night, congratulations, and *Auf Wiedersehen.*"

* * *

When Bobby came back from the bathroom, Ann was already in bed reading. As he lay down and pulled the blanket over him, Ann said, "Here is one more good story, which I happened to open up on. Listen to this one!"

"A certain man went down from Jerusalem to Jericho and fell among thieves, which stripped him of his raiment and wounded him and departed, leaving him half dead. But a certain Samaritan, as he journeyed, came where he was. And when he saw him, he had compassion with him. And he went to him and bound up his wounds, pouring in oil and wine, and set him on his own beast, and brought him to an inn, and took care of him. And on the morrow, when he departed, he took out two pence and gave them to the host and said onto him, 'Take care of him, and whatever thou spendest more, I will repay thee.'"

Bobby remained silent while studying the ceiling. At length he replied, "There was another great human being . . . And you know, Ann, you are a great human being yourself. The best! I love you even more than the day we were married." He drew himself closer and kissed her . . .

* * *

Chapter 13

McClures' Vacation in the Old Country

The next morning, the two McClure families slept until past eight, and when they finally entered the hotel's restaurant for breakfast, most of the customers had already finished eating. Over the bacon and eggs, they discussed their options for their second and last sightseeing day in London.

Helen had a collection of pamphlets from the hotel's tourist desk, offering various bus excursions. They at length agreed on a guided tour to "Famous Castles, Gardens, and Estates in Southern England," which included lunch and dinner at 'picturesque and historical village inns.' The tour was scheduled to leave the hotel at 10 a.m. and returning at about 9 p.m. Helen immediately went to the tourist desk to place reservations and came back reporting that she had booked the last available seats on the tour.

Comfortably seated in the large sightseeing bus, they left the hotel in bright sunshine. The first stop was at Cardinal Wolsey's Hampton Court, after about half an hour's driving. Their tour guide took them on a walk through the buildings and the adjoining

Dutch Gardens and Bushey Park. Next, they stopped for lunch at a quaint-looking village restaurant on their way to New Windsor. In the early afternoon, they arrived at Windsor Castle in Berkshire, part of which dated back to the ninth century, where they again exited the bus to walk to the Round Tower, St. George's Chapel, the Horseshoe Cloister, besides visiting the Royal Mew, the Home Park, and Frogmore, the latter being the final resting place for Queen Victoria and Prince Albert.

Later in the afternoon, they drove to Buckinghamshire, visiting old country homes, parks, and gardens: Cliveden Estate, Hampden Estate, Chequers Country House, Ascott, Waddledon Manor, and Hughenden House. At half past six, they stopped at another picturesque old restaurant in West Wycombe Village, where they had a hearty meal, doubly appreciated after the many long walks.

It was still twilight when the bus returned to the Dorchester Hotel and unloaded its cargo of tired, but happy, tourists. The four McClures agreed to retire early in order to be ready for the journey to Scotland the following day.

* * *

The next day, the McClure family took a taxi to Victoria Station, and then the 10:15 a.m. train to Edinburgh, Scotland. Here they rented an Austin car, and for the following nine days, they leisurely toured the length and breath of Scotland.

Over the narrow winding roads in hilly terrain, they drove from Edinburgh, around the Firth of Forth to Kirkcaldy, outside of where Bobby's grandfather Donald McClure had been born, the fourth child of farmers Andrew and Aime McClure. They spent three days in Kirkcaldy, searching the church register, which confirmed that Donald had been born on October 5, 1867, and baptized in the church on March 18, 1868. A faded ink note in the margin stated that Donald had emigrated to America in 1890, address unknown.

When they tried to locate the small McClure farm, they found that the dwelling had been torn down and the fields incorporated in a larger neighboring farm. The new owner was most hospitable and showed the fields that had formerly belonged to the McClure farm, including the foundations of the old farmhouse and a newer barn which had been built in the 1930s on the same location. They were invited to spend the evening with the farmer's family and were treated like royalty. After dinner and a few glasses of Scotch malt whiskey, the farmer and one of his sons brought out their bagpipes and gave a demonstration of authentic Scotch bag piping. It became another memorable evening with the singing of old Scotch folk songs and lively talking. Unfortunately, the farmer had no information on the whereabouts of the present McClure generation. It was past midnight before the McClures, to the singing of "Auld Lang Syne," got back to their rented car and rumbled to their hotel in Kirkcaldy.

Using the telephone directory, they called or visited some of the many McClures in the Kirkcaldy area. An elderly retired butcher was the only person who could trace his ancestors back to the old farmstead. His father had been a brother to Bobby's grandfather.

The years had weakened the old butcher's memory, but after a few whiskeys, he did recall that his father had talked several times about his brother Donald in America. Donald had apparently worked on his father's farm until he was nearly twenty-three years old but had then decided to emigrate with his wife and first child to the United States, where they had hoped to get their own farm. The butcher's father had also mentioned that Donald had married a lovely lassie, who had been the daughter of family friends from the other side of the firth.

The butcher searched for a long time among a large collection of old letters he had inherited from his father, but unfortunately, he could not find any correspondence from Donald McClure.

Continuing their sightseeing, they drove up to Dundee, Aberdeen, and over to Inverness at the entrance to Loch Ness. The driving further north to Sutherland was a particular challenge but well worth it, they agreed. Traveling down the craggy west coast was an exercise in stamina and patience. In Torridon, they were able to board a trawler that took them on a cruise along the rugged cliffs and islands in the North Minch.

South of Lake Locky, the roads improved again. They spent two days in Glasgow, studying the rich heritage of that large city before finally motoring back to the International Hotel at Heathrow Airport outside of London.

* * *

Chapter 14

My Bonnie is over the Ocean

Under a clear blue mid-June sky, they could see the outline of the Irish Sea, with Wales behind them and the Isle of Man on their right. The Irish coastline was dimly visible ahead. The Boeing 747 airplane was still climbing towards its cruising altitude for the flight across the Atlantic Ocean.

With a satisfied smile, Bobby McClure, on an impulse, took his wife's hand in his and began humming the tune of 'My Bonnie is over the Ocean.' Ann looked puzzled at him for a moment and then joined him in the humming on the third line. "Bring back . . . bring back. Oh bring back my Bonnie to me, to me . . ."

"You know, Ann, sitting up here surely changes one's whole perspective. Flying is like taking an escalator to a high mountain top, from where you can face eternity. There is a vast horizon all around you, and the world is laid out orderly and held in good balance. Right now, we are probably at about the same elevation as the summit of Mount Everest. I think that I now understand what the wife of that illusionist we met in London, Señor Fontini, meant by *stimmung*, when she referred to the influence of mountains on her state of mind. I really feel at ease up here."

"I know what you mean! I can feel it too," replied Ann.

"But don't you think that one can feel *stimmung* in most places? Do you, for example, remember that evening we were invited to dinner by the farmer outside of Kirkcaldy? I had the same feeling then when I heard the bagpipes played by those hospitable and skillful people. No sour notes, perfect teamwork, timing, and harmony. They are proud people with a lust for living, freely expressing their inner feelings, and trying to do their very best in everything they do. I really fell in love with those people in Scotland."

A new smile came over Bobby McClure's face, and he continued, "I do suppose that I have come to feel a certain kinship with the people of Scotland now that I better know where I came from. And frankly, I am a little prouder too because of it. Can't you see that I am all puffed up? I am probably going to be one of the most insufferable, nostalgic, expatriate Scots in Boone County."

"Yes, it was a good idea," replied Ann.

"A good idea?"

"What you suggested. Having this vacation. Have you forgotten that it was your idea?"

"Yes, I suppose that it was a good idea. I am glad that I thought of it and that you agreed. And also that Stafford and Helen could join us. And we didn't have a flat tire this time," chuckled Bobby.

"Now that you mentioned that illusionist, there is one thing that I am still wondering about," Ann said.

"And what could that be?"

"Were you really serious when you, in so many words, hinted that the Fontinis or perhaps I should say, the Schneiders, made the six hikers on the Watauga Overlook forget their supposed involvement in the demise of the four motorcyclists?"

"I take it that you already have found out that the German word 'Schneider' translates into 'Taylor' in English? Was I serious? You have always been better in the intuition department than I am. What do you think?" countered Bobby evasively.

"Based on their own admission, the Fontinis might have been in the area that year and maybe even at that time. We have to underline 'perhaps,' mind you! They certainly appear to have the capacity to do what you described, and they seemed to have the right instincts for acting in that fashion. Yes, I think that you were being very serious. But why did you insist on asking them, Bobby?"

Bobby shrugged his shoulders. "To be honest, I don't know. I certainly did not want to make them feel guilty or uncomfortable, but there is a little bit of a Sherlock Holmes in every good law-enforcement person. It's in our blood! However, did I not accept your derailment that the whole scenario was too circumstantial, that there are no conclusive proofs whatsoever, and that it in general is incredible?"

"So, do you mean to say that you admit that your point of view was built on far-fetched or well neigh baseless hunches only, or were you really expecting that the Fontinis would make a confession right then and there?"

"I believe that I was so caught up in the realization that it is possible to selectively erase memories, of which I had no prior knowledge. I then added two and two and saw in a flash a perfectly logical explanation of what might have taken place on that overlook, a mysterious case that had been boggling our department's collective brains silly for many months. Honestly, Ann, I decided on the spur of the moment to see what kind of reaction I would get from the Fontinis if I exposed it. But, as you heard, they neither confirmed nor denied that they had been present on the overlook that day. What does that show?"

"At face value, it shows me that they were polite listeners, who did not want to embarrass you by pointing out that you did not have any right to interrogate them, whether or not they had been on the overlook!"

"Your point is well taken. But, my dear Dr. Watson, apart from that, you must admit that my speculation is not all that far-fetched, based on what is known now. It is simply the only way the pieces of the puzzle will fall into place. I am as confident now as I was when I outlined my hypothesis at the table in the Terrace Room of the Dorchester Hotel two weeks ago that it is the only possible explanation of what actually took place on the Watauga Overlook that Tuesday in early June of 1975."

"Oh, come on now, Bobby. That is easy to say, but you have still not convinced me! Would you please tell me why you can 'feel' all that certain?" challenged Ann.

"Well, for starters, I never could accept that the four motorcyclists had not arrived on the overlook until after half past three in the afternoon. All available facts support the view that they should have arrived several hours earlier. Such as the time they disappeared from the highway, the distance between the parked motorcycles and the overlook, their obvious motive for wanting to know the activities on the highway, their expertise in outdoor living, including a good understanding of weather patterns, and especially the necessity of explaining that there was a hot fire present that caused Firebird's burns. However, with four or six respected citizens willing to swear that the motorcyclists had not shown up before they departed at about that time, we were forced to accept the later time frame for the arrival of the motorcyclists on the overlook, which the grand jury used as the basis for their decision. In doing so, the jury virtually eliminated the possibility that others could have been involved in their deaths, as all those known to have been in the vicinity had been accounted for, and logistically could not have been on the overlook during the later time frame. However, having accepted that conclusion a Pandora's box of unanswerable questions opened regarding how it was possible that every one of the four motorcyclists could have died within a short span of time, and their bodies later discovered together with their belongings in the jumble a hundred feet below the overlook, without leaving any traces of a fight.

"On the other hand, if we had assumed that the Henderson hiking party had not spoken the truth about meeting with the riders, no person in his right mind would even remotely suspect that they could have been involved in eliminating the four motorcyclists. And certainly, if they had tried to do so against all odds, one would expect that there would have been at least some serious injuries among them. But we knew that when they returned from their hiking trip, they were all healthy and in good spirits. They could, of course, have lied about their departure time from the overlook. But, if they had a part in putting the four motorcyclists away, what motive could they have had for falsifying their departure time. I can't think of any. Their risk of being involved in an investigation would have been exactly the same. They simply chose to tell the truth, as they remembered it. So there was no reason to even suspect that they had anything to do with the deaths of the motorcycle riders," concluded Bobby.

"Maybe it was my participation in Fontini's act that triggered your imagination?" asked Ann.

"Probably . . . yes! Together with another incident that happened that same day in London. Memory erasing would explain why the Henderson group did not recall having met with the hoodlums. It is, of course, conceivable that there are other illusionists in the world who are capable of performing a similar act. But that evening, I thought that I remembered that it was Señor Fontini, alias Mr. Schneider, alias Mr. Taylor, that I saw coming out with the Henderson party in the parking lot that late afternoon in 1975. He looks a little older now, but the profile and his movements are the same."

Bobby continued, "But you almost stopped me in my tracks, Ann, when you declared that evening that my explanation couldn't be true, because if any entertainer had been able to achieve such a spectacular feat offstage, in your opinion, they would certainly have made sure that it was hyped up in the media for purposes of self-promotion. As they had not done so, could it be that they themselves had unlawful activities to hide? In theory, they too could have participated in the battle against the motorcyclists, or they may have been involved in illicit trade of some kind? However, as they were chance tourists in a remote region of a foreign country, between professional engagements, and had no personal ties to anyone in the Henderson group, I find it exceedingly unlikely that it could have been the reason for their silence. We spent almost two hours socializing with them at the hotel. They may be evasive on this particular subject, but my firm impression is that they are stable individuals and dependable citizens. The only motive for their silence I can think of is that they are shielding the hikers. Can you think of any other motives, Ann?"

"No, I can't think of any. I agree that compassion and kindness would fit their personal characteristics," admitted Ann.

"So, logically, they must have been attempting to undo emotional traumas suffered by at least some of the hikers. When I looked at that tableau or display in Madame Tussaud's Chamber of Horror in London on the first day of our vacation, showing Jack the Ripper stabbing one of his victims, I somehow came to think of SS's fatal knife wound. It was definitely not made in the same fashion. That same evening, it suddenly dawned on me that SS must have been lying on top of his murderer or murderess at the moment he was stabbed. That would have to be the only relative position conforming with the orientation and position of the knife in SS's back. To me it always seemed improbable that the murderer could have been one of the other motorcyclists, and I can't explain why we didn't make that deduction in the original investigation. If you add SS's documented history of sex offenses, it should adequately explain at least one serious trauma."

"And why do you think that Mrs. Henderson was SS's victim rather than Mrs. Wannamaker?" wondered Ann.

"Chiefly because she gave me the impression of having more emotional depth, based on the brief conversations I had with them. Also, she would probably have felt more remorseful after having stabbed her assailant due to her religious devotion. And, additionally, the boys' desperate decision to attack the vicious intruders probably was triggered when her son witnessed his mother's plight. However, even if it had been Mrs. Wannamaker, whom SS was attempting to rape, it would not have changed the scenario in substance," replied Bobby.

"Yes, I can accept that. But how are you able to deduce the course of the rescue efforts by the boys?"

"From several available facts. First, as I have mentioned before, we found pieces of freshly cut knotted ropes under two of the trees on the southwestern fringe of the overlook, the commercial quality of which matched a length of rope we found in one of Firebird's pockets. Someone must have cut them after the knots had been tied. Second, during an interview with Mr. Wannamaker in Hickory, we learned about his and the boys' involvement in Little League Baseball. And thirdly, Mrs. Henderson at the same occasion made an off-the-cuff remark about Howie's disappointment because Eric had failed to take him to the mountain spring that day, as previously promised. It's a short step to visualize that most of the many bruises on High Command's body was caused by stoning rather than from falling. And likewise to attribute Howie's disappointment of not being shown the spring to his memory loss caused by the collective memory erazing. In any case, it is inconceivable that any sane, mature adult would have dared to launch an assault on those unpredictable and hardened criminals."

Bobby McClure chuckled as he continued. "The coming together of all these different pieces probably was most fortuitous though. We were both a little off the ground from jet lag, celebration and wine. What worries me most is that perhaps it was Mr. Fontini who put all that stuff in my head. You know, he seems to be able to do just about everything!"

"No, Bobby, my dear. I think that I owe you an apology. I have to admit that your deductions are well thought out and fits together seamlesssly. I believe that I called your hypothesis 'incredible' after you explained it that evening. I probably did not pay enough attention to grasp many of the clues and details you just mentioned. Or maybe I felt sorry for the Fontinis because you used their act in your scenario and thought that you were pressing them to confess?" Ann looked genuinely sorry.

"Don't you worry, Ann. There is no reason to apologize for that! As usual, you were right in using that word 'incredible.' That's a most fitting description for what took place, don't you agree?"

"So we have lived long enough to see the perfect crime taking place right under our own noses, albeit in the name of compassion," mused Ann.

"You could say that, in a manner of speaking. But without a confession from the Fontinis, we shall never be sure. There simply is no other way of proving my hypothesis. If they really wanted to make a confession, they could do it now without fear of being prosecuted, as the ten-year statutory limit has expired. However, just to set things straight, in case I am mistaken, I shall write them a personal letter after we return and relieve them of all suspicion."

"The funny thing is that now I am convinced that your explanation has to be accurate. Why did I not understand sooner that the Fontinis took this burden on themselves to help the six hikers overcome the hurt and damage the hoodlums had brought into their lives? Even when it meant that they could never mention their involvement! Were the actual happenings ever to be known by the hikers, the pains and self-incriminations would be inflicted once more. No, I definitely think that you should never mention your tale again. Write a friendly letter to the Fontinis, but do not make any allusions to your hypothesis. They will understand you."

"Ann! How did I ever deserve to be married to you? You are simply marvelous. And you are also absolutely right. All this shall remain an unspoken secret between us and the Fontinis."

After a brief pause, Bobby continued, "Ann there is another matter I would like to have your input on. You know that my term of office as county sheriff expires in three years. How would you feel if I did not run for reelection to that office?"

"That's entirely up to you, Bobby. Do you think that you have incriminated yourself by having decided to keep your hypothesis to yourself?"

"No, Ann, there is no connection. We have already agreed that there is no basis for reopening that old case. But I have been doing some thinking lately, and this may be a good time for me to prepare some changes. The sheriff's department is in good hands and running well. I should like to see Wilson having a chance to become the next sheriff. He has the aptitude and the interest, and he is also an outstanding individual. He is forty-four years old now and should not have to wait much longer."

Bobby continued, "As you know, I have been on the executive committee of the party for the past eight years. It so happens that Theodore Murwell, the state senator from our district, has decided that he does not want to run for another term. He is getting up in years and thinks that it may be time for him to retire from active politics. The party nominating committee has asked if I might be interested in running for Murwell's seat in 1988? I am aware that I have never been elected to be a public representative before, but I think that I would fit in quite nicely, and I do have a number of ideas I should like to advocate in the Senate. I also believe that the constituency of the district is supporting most of them, but they need a spokesman.

"And lastly, I think that I have locked up more than my quota of people in my time! Like the Fontinis, I should like to work on keeping our people freer and happier for a change."

Ann looked earnestly at her husband, studying his face. At length she replied, "If your heart is in it, do it!"

Bobby squeezed Ann's hand lightly. "You are the greatest of all lassies, Ann. Then I am going to risk it. I just made up my mind."

"That sounds great, Governor. We are 200 percent behind you," answered Ann with a twinkle in her eye.

"I take you overseas for two weeks and you already speak like a Limey! Senator! For now it is senator. One step at a time. But who knows, we may consider that possibility some other day, darling?" Bobby looked quite content with himself.

The big airplane had reached the cruising altitude and leveled off. Accompanied by the muffled whine from the four turbine engines, Bobby and Ann, hand in hand, resumed their humming of 'My Bonnie is over the Ocean.'

* * *

Postscript

The events and characters depicted in this novel are purely fictional. Any perceived similarity between the novel's characters and real persons, dead or alive, is coincidental and unintended by the author. For effects, some minor changes in geographical, organizational, and administrative details have been included in the novel.

BVG